Other titles by

JANET DAILEY
IN HARLEQUIN PRESENTS

Many of these titles, and other titles in the
Harlequin Romance series, are available at your
local bookseller or through the Harlequin Reader
Service. For a free catalogue listing all available
Harlequin Presents and Harlequin Romances,
send your name and address to:

HARLEQUIN READER SERVICE,
M.P.O. Box 707,
Niagara Falls, N.Y. 14302
Canadian address:
Stratford, Ontario, Canada N5A 6W2
or use order coupon at back of book.

JANET DAILEY

sonora sundown

Harlequin Books

TORONTO • LONDON • NEW YORK • AMSTERDAM • SYDNEY

Harlequin Presents edition published June 1978
ISBN 0-373-70739-8

Original hardcover edition published in 1978
by Mills & Boon Limited

CHAPTER ONE

A WHISPER OF GOLD danced over the sage, the first promise of sundown. The tufted heads of grass bowed their acceptance as the evening breeze stirred with a rustling yawn.

A road runner darted along a parallel course with the gray Arabian gelding as it stepped lightly over the gravelly sand base. The roadrunner swerved abruptly to the cover of some mesquite and disappeared. The touch of the rein against the side of the sleek gray neck altered the horse's direction to the right where the broad flatness of a bare rock held back the desert plants from its section of sloping land.

Metal horseshoes clinked on bare rock. There Brandy Ames checked her mount to a halt and gazed at the unobstructed view the position gave her. A gray ear swivelled toward her. The horse stretched its neck in protest against the tightened rein and impatiently tossed its head.

Cream yellow had begun to encroach on the blue sky. Fingers of orange spread out from the western horizon, changing the color of the shadows cast by the setting sun; even the short curls of Brandy's honey-gold hair had a copper hue.

"I wish I were an artist and could paint a picture as glorious as this." Absently she petted the sleek neck, speaking aloud her thoughts to the horse from long habit. "It changes so magically, though. It's like watching in slow-motion as a flower bud opens into a beautiful bloom." The horse snorted and Brandy laughed softly. "Am I being too fanciful, Rashad? As we get to know each other better, you'll find that I tend to get carried away by the Arizona sunsets."

Looping the end of the reins around the horn of her western saddle, Brandy dismounted with springing lightness, moving with unconscious grace to the head of her mount. There she stopped, spying the first crimson pink strokes that touched the thin trail of clouds scattered about the sky.

A pale golden tan glowed from her sunny features. Round, brightly luminous eyes of turquoise-green were accented by the turned-up tip of her nose and the delicately perfect outline of her mouth. Slightly built, there was a deceptive air of fragility about her that neglected notice of her medium height in favor of slender wrist and ankle bones. The inherent animation in her looks made Brandy attractive, yet the watchful stillness that was for ever about her kept her in the background.

If asked, Brandy would have laughed at the idea she might be shy, but there was an air of reserve about her that few had penetrated. Now she was alone and there was no need to be reserved. So she cast it aside.

The horse nudged her shoulder as if reminding her of his presence. In answer, she stroked his face without taking her eyes from the budding sunset.

"Today at the shop Karen was bragging about the magnificence of the Rocky Mountains, how rugged and splendorous they were." A contented sigh accompanied her remark. "She's welcome to all that craggy grandeur, Rashad, and I'll just keep right on falling in love with the Sonora Desert every day at sundown!"

The foothills of the mountains blazed a crimson-orange, set afire by the ball of flame dipping near the earth. The vast expanse of blue sky to the east now displayed a purple cast while the western horizon became an intense red-orange. Her breath was caught by the vibrant splash of color. Her hand trailed away from the horse's face, down to the velvet softness of his nose, then to her side.

The gray nuzzled her shoulder again, impatiently blowing through his nose as his shod hooves shifted restlessly on the barren wind- and sand-smoothed rock.

"Stop thinking about your stomach, Rashad." Brandy tapped his nose smartly when the horse displayed an inclination to nibble the sleeve of her white blouse. "Your oats and hay will still be at the stable when we get back. No one else is going to eat them. Just look at this sunset!" Her hand arced toward the horizon. "You're going to have to learn to enjoy this the way Star did. She kept me company over many a sandwich supper eaten in the desert twilight."

As always the memory of the pinto mare brought a wistful sadness to the corners of her mouth. From the

7

time she could remember as a child, Brandy had wanted a horse, but not until she was ten years old did her parents give in and present her with an eight-year-old pinto mare. They had been an inseparable pair until age finally claimed the mare last summer, a week after Brandy's twentieth birthday.

Rashad, the spirited Arabian gelding beside her, had been purchased this past winter after a dutiful mourning period for the mare, her childhood playmate and friend. Brandy still found it difficult not to make comparisons between the two horses, so totally different in personality.

But Brandy supposed it was natural that at times she did compare the two. Star had been such a vital part of her childhood, a friend, a playmate, a confidant of all her secrets. Not that she hadn't had school friends, because she had. It was just that living here in the country west of Tucson, without any neighbors near enough to count, and an only child, Brandy had come to rely very much on the companionship of her horse.

As she grew up, she had been alone a lot but had never considered herself lonely. Her parents' love and affection had been constant, even if sometimes they marveled that Brandy was actually their child. Both Lenora and Stewart Ames had doctorate degrees in their particular field of study and had professorships at the University of Tucson. Career-minded, they were initially surprised by Brandy's lack of ambition.

Yet their love and wisdom was such that they never tried to force her to follow any particular path. If she preferred pottering around the house and working with her hands, then they were happy in her contentment. If they were ever disappointed because she hadn't chosen to pursue an intellectual path, they didn't show it.

Never once had Brandy felt less than an equal to them because she held an undemanding position as a clerk in an arts and crafts shop and handled most of the household duties. It was true that at twenty, nearly twenty-one, she was a little slow at leaving the nest.

Karen, her closest friend and the girl she worked with at the shop, had urged Brandy to move into Tucson and share an apartment with her. But that would have meant giving up Rashad and the serenity of stepping out of the house into the desert, miles from anywhere, with no other buildings to mar the view of the awesome stretch of sand and sage and sky.

And the sunsets. How she would miss the sunsets if she lived in the city, Brandy sighed. Sometimes she was content to view them from the shelter of the patio behind her ranch-style home. Other times, like now, she felt compelled to ride several miles into the desert to witness this silent eulogy to nature.

Wandering to the edge of the flat rock as if to move closer to the blazing red-orange that claimed the sky, she breathed in deeply. The air around her was cool and still. Soon she would have to slip on the tightly-woven denim jacket tied to the back of her saddle, but right now the faint crispness was a refreshing change from the afternoon's warmth.

"How spectacular it is," she murmured. "And no sunset is exactly like the ones that came before. It's like a magic kaleidoscope in the sky."

Behind her, there was a pawing of horseshoe against stone, rasping and metallic. Brandy glanced over her shoulder, turquoise eyes dancing to the impatient gray.

"Now if Dad was here, he would give you a very scientific explanation as to why earth has such boldly ostentatious sunsets," she grinned. "You see, Rashad, it all has to do with the earth's atmosphere and the way it filters the light from the sun. The reason the sun seems so intensely bright at noontime is because that's when the light is subjected to the least amount of filtering by the atmosphere because the sun is directly overhead. However, at sunrise and sunset, the sunlight has to travel through more of the atmosphere and the violet, blue and green colors are filtered out, while allowing the reds and yellows and oranges to come through. Further," Brandy continued her mock lecture, "the sunsets are more brilliantly painted because of the amount of dust particles that are suspended in the atmosphere during the daylight hours."

The overall hue of the western horizon deepened to a crimson shade. Brandy hooked her thumbs through the belt loops of her levis and sighed.

"It takes away some of the magic, doesn't it, when you start describing a sunset with words like light rays and filters and atmosphere." She tipped her head to one side in contemplation, feathery curls of honey gold framing her face. "It's much more enjoyable when there's mystery in the wonder of it."

The hush that followed her thoughtful words was broken by a rifle report. Some rancher shooting at a coyote, Brandy started to shrug it off, knowing how far sound carried in the desert, but the cracking explosion wasn't dismissed by the fitful Arabian.

On the heels of the rifle shot came the clattering of hooves on stone, and Brandy whirled around to see the bunching hindquarters of her horse as Rashad bolted toward home. Her first reaction was instinctive. She put two fingers to her mouth and whistled shrilly. Star would have responded to the call immediately, but to the Arabian it meant nothing.

"Rashad!" Brandy started racing after the galloping horse, the graveled earth hampering her attempt to run. "Rashad! Come back here."

But within a few feet, she knew she didn't stand a chance of catching the horse. Even at a distance she could see the arched neck and the ears pricked forward. He was heading home to the stable and the oats and hay. She doubted if he would slow to less than a canter the whole way back.

"You just wait," Brandy muttered, cursing beneath her breath at the total absence of loyalty. "You dumb, stupid—"

11

There was no need to blame the horse. She ran her fingers wearily through her hair. The fault was hers for not ground-hitching the reins. She deserved the long walk home for being so careless. It was time she recognized that Rashad was not the dependable Star.

At least there was consolation in knowing that her parents had gone out for the evening and they wouldn't be alarmed when Rashad returned without her. Balancing that were the ever-lengthening shadows and the increasing coolness of the air.

On horseback, the five or more miles she had traveled would seem like nothing, but on foot in this terrain it was going to be a very long and cold walk. And a hungry one, too, Brandy thought regretfully, as she remembered the sandwiches tucked in the saddlebags.

She turned for one last look at the deepened red of the sunset. The golden glow of the sun had dipped below the horizon, and the first evening star glittered faintly in the purpling sky. Now the darkness would come with a suddenness. It was a sobering thought to travel the miles home on foot, totally alone and in the dark.

Squaring her shoulders, Brandy started in the direction of home. It was strange how different the land looked when not viewed from the top of a horse. The mesquite and sage seemed thicker and the sloping hill appeared steeper. There was a momentary qualm as she wondered how much different it would look in total darkness, then she thrust the vague fear away.

Briskly she increased her pace. There was the reassuring knowledge that within a couple of miles, or three at the most, she would be able to see the light on the stable roof. It would be a beacon to guide her the last miles home.

So she walked. One minute she was aware of the long shadows and the next there was blackness. The moon was only a tiny sliver in the night sky, its light next to worthless. Stars shimmered dimly, fairy dust that was pretty but not illuminating.

The only sound seemed to be her footsteps crunching through the combination of sand and gravel and the brushing of her levis against the sage and mesquite. It was difficult to avoid the patches of prickly pear cactus. Often she walked into them, discovering too late that the dark mound was not sage-brush. Then she would be forced to backtrack a few steps and skirt the thorny desert plant.

Of necessity, her attention was directed on the ground ahead of her. It was impossible to keep her points of reference in focus at all times. Whenever she stopped to catch her breath, she would quickly scan ahead of her to locate them again. Several times she thought she had lost them, but always she had found them and would start out again.

It was too dark to read the hands on her watch, but Brandy had been positive that at the top of the third knoll she would have been able to see the stable light. She studied the beautiful night sky and the brightening stars.

Could it possibly get much darker? she asked herself. A wry grimace crossed her mouth. It was a pity she hadn't listened more attentively when her father had tried to explain the position of the stars and constellations. She might have been able to use that knowledge to verify her directions.

"Maybe that tall clump of mesquite is blocking the light," she murmured aloud, and trudged forward.

She had no idea how far she had walked already. It seemed like miles, but it probably wasn't. She was beginning to get winded. The temperature had dropped several degrees and she shivered uncontrollably at the cold.

Her head throbbed dully. Brandy blamed it on the increasing hunger pangs in her stomach. When she got home, she intended to have an enormous bowl of that beef stew that was in the refrigerator. The tantilizing picture that formed in her mind didn't lessen the gnawing emptiness within.

About a thousand steps later, she stopped kidding herself. Nothing around her looked even vaguely familiar. Somewhere, somehow, she had turned around. Exhausted and feeling slightly weak from hunger, she sank to her knees, unmindful of the sharp pebbles that bit into her flesh. She was lost.

The next question was how far off-course was she? And should she continue on in the hope that she would sight some landmark that would give her the necessary bearings to find her way home? This wasn't the first time she had found herself lost in the desert.

The difference was that before she had always left it up to Star to find their way home when Brandy's haphazard system of navigating had failed.

It was impossible that she could have wandered too far in the wrong direction, she told herself firmly. She rubbed her hands briskly over the gooseflesh that seemed to have permanently dimpled her bare arms. If she continued straight ahead, sooner or later she would either see the lights of her home or run into the graveled road that led to the neighboring ranch house.

She would continue on, she decided. Movement was definitely better than sitting in one place freezing to death. A slight exaggeration, she admitted, since it was unlikely it would get that cold. She knew that the general advice was for a person to stay in one place if they became lost. But she wasn't aimlessly wandering about. She was going forward on a straight path that should either lead her within sight of her home or the graveled road that would eventually bring her to it.

She hadn't traveled very far when she developed a stitch in her side. Pausing, she pressed a hand against the pain and looked around. Off to her left, she thought she had seen the flicker of a light. She had been positive her home was either straight ahead or to the right.

Silently she stood studying the area where she thought she had seen the light, trying to force her eyes to pierce the darkness and the shadowy desert growth. Then she saw it again, wavering and fading, but definitely a light of some sort, she thought gladly.

With new purpose, Brandy set out toward it. This time she paid less attention to where she was putting her feet. A light in the desert had to mean people, although she doubted it was her home.

As she drew closer, fighting the sage and cactus that whipped at her legs, her thick leather boots taking the brunt of the punishment, the light became more definite. Then it suddenly took shape. It was a campfire sheltered in the notch of a hill, probably only visible from her direction. Brandy wanted to laugh at the luck that had smiled on her, but she was too weary to do more than grin breathlessly.

"Hello!" She ran toward the fire, an inner relief bringing a note of gaiety into her voice.

At the edge of the circle of light, a dark form moved at her call, the builder of the fire and her rescuer. The shape stayed in the curtain of shadows as Brandy burst into the ring of light opposite him.

"Boy, am I glad to see you!" she declared with a laughing trill of relief. "Somehow or other I got lost on my way home. I was beginning to think I was going to spend the night on the desert alone."

"Really?" The male voice was low and husky, sharp with a quiet kind of anger.

A slight frown drew Brandy's eyebrows together. She hadn't expected an open-armed welcome, but she had thought the man would express concern when she explained that she was lost.

"I ... I was out riding." She decided a further ex-

16

planation must be necessary. "My horse bolted. I was walking home when it got dark. That's when I must have got my directions turned around."

There was a pulsing second of silence before the man in the shadows responded. "And you just stumbled into my camp by chance, is that it?" Again hard, cynical mockery lined the low voice.

"I saw the light from your campfire," she spoke hesitantly, trying to peer through the darkness to see more than a dark human shape. A horse stamped in the darkness, and Brandy could feel perspiration gathering in the palms of her hands. "It was such a welcome sight."

Unconsciously she used the past tense. All of a sudden, she didn't feel so very lucky. Who was this man, and what was he doing out here in the middle of the desert?

The fire burned through a thick branch, sending the two parts crumbling into the center. Flames flared brightly at the new fuel, light radiating into a bigger arc that encompassed the man. Something shiny flashed in his hand, and fear welled into a huge knot in Brandy's throat at the menacing knife-blade.

Her gaze ricocheted to his face. The wide brim of his stetson hat was pulled low, hiding all but the narrowed glitter of his eyes. A dark, shaggy growth of hair covered his jaw, check, and chin. It was too long to be unshaven stubble, yet not quite a beard either.

A lined suede vest covered the dark shirt he wore and accented the broadness of his shoulders. Faded levis fitted snugly over his hips and thighs. In the flickering firelight, he seemed much larger than Brandy had realized, larger and somehow frightening.

His disreputable appearance did nothing to reassure her. The man had made it obvious that he didn't care that she had got herself lost. His only concern seemed to be that she had stumbled into his camp.

He was angered that she had found him. That could only mean he wasn't supposed to be here. Brandy swallowed tightly. Was the man a cattle rustler? That seemed a logical conclusion, since they had become more of a plague than they ever had been in the Old West days. The more she considered the possibility the more certain she became that she was right.

He wasn't a cowboy from the neighboring ranch; she had a nodding acquaintance with most of them. In this modern day and age of trailering horses and four-wheel vehicles, it was rare that a working cowboy ever had a camp out on the range. Whatever this man's purpose was, Brandy was certain it was no good.

What kind of a position did that put her in? She had seen him. She knew he was camped here. What was more, she could identify him.

A cold finger of fear trailed down her spine as her gaze was drawn back to the knife held in the hand at his side. She could identify him if she got out of this alive, she realized with chilling terror.

"Look, I don't want to be any trouble." Her voice wavered thinly. "If you could just give me directions to the Ames house, I'll be on my way."

18

"You will, will you?" he returned with sardonic amusement. White teeth flashed in the dark beard growth as his upper lip curled over the words. "You could get lost again?" The glittering light in his eyes seemed to indicate that he found that possibility humorous.

But Brandy knew what he really meant. He had no intention of letting her leave. Panic started to engulf her. When the man took a step forward, she knew she had only one chance.

With a gasping cry of fear, she pivoted and raced back into the desert. Panicked, she didn't care which direction she ran, only that it was away from the fire and the man. There was no sound of pursuit, but she was making so much noise that she doubted if she could hear him chasing her.

Her blind flight carried her on a path through thickets of chaparral. Thorny bushes and cactus tore at her blouse and skin and the thick growth and uneven ground impeded her progress to a stumbling run that required more exertion to cover a small amount of ground.

Then she tripped. A startled cry was ripped from her throat as she was pitched headlong forward, hitting the ground with a force that momentarily knocked the wind out of her. Gasping for air, she rolled on to her back, unmindful of the prickly brush beneath her. Her eyes blinked open to focus on the tall man looming above her. For a full second she couldn't move.

19

"That was a stupid thing to do," he said in a sigh that was tinged with exasperation.

He started to bend toward her and Brandy cringed closer to the ground. "Don't touch me!" For all her inner fear, her voice rang defiantly clear.

"Shut up!" He shook his head and reached down to haul her unceremoniously to her feet.

Immediately she began twisting and kicking to be free of the iron grip of his fingers. She struggled furiously, and her boot finally connected with his shinbone.

"You little bitch!" he muttered beneath his breath. "What the hell are you trying to prove?"

With unbelievable swiftness, her wrists were captured in one hand and she was lifted off the ground, tucked beneath one arm and balanced on his hips. Her feet continued to kick the air as he carried her as effortlessly as if she had been a sack of potatoes back towards the fire.

"Let me down or I'll scream!" Brandy demanded in a throbbing voice.

"By all means, scream if you want," the man countered smoothly. "Maybe all the rattlesnakes and scorpions will come charging to your rescue."

The realization that no one would hear her cries for help only made her struggle more vigorously against the iron band that pinned her hands and held her easily off the ground. By the time they reached the circle of the campfire he hadn't lessened his grip one inch. There he set her roughly on her feet.

The instant he released her, she started to run back to the safety of the desert, only to be brought up short by hard fingers that dug into the soft flesh of her shoulders and pulled back against the solid wall of his chest.

"Let me go!" she hissed violently.

"Lost, huh?" he mocked harshly against her ear. "Or do you have some friends on the other side of the hill?"

"No," Brandy protested with genuine confusion, "I told you I was lost. No one's with me, I swear."

Too late she realized that she had made a mistake. If he had thought someone was waiting for her nearby, he might have been reluctant to harm her. Now he had no reason for caution.

Terror gave her a fresh surge of strength to renew her flight to escape. Using her elbows and heels, she struck out at him. At the same time, she twisted and writhed to break the bruising grip of his hands. Her breath came in panting sobs of desperation.

"I'm not going to put up with these hysterics much longer," he growled.

Somehow she managed to hook her foot behind his leg and knock him off balance. His hold lessened but he still managed to drag her to the ground with him. Before she could roll free, he was on top of her, the crushing weight of his body holding her down. With a muffled cry, Brandy tried to gouge at his glittering dark eyes with her fingernails, but they never got close to their target.

In a flash both arms were stretched out on the ground above her head, her wrists pinned by his hands. Helplessly trapped, she continued trying to twist from beneath the male length of him. He was too heavy and too strong.

"Are you going to stop this?" he snapped. "You're only proving what a little fool you are!"

She paused to catch her breath. Her head was twisted as far to the side as it could go, her eyes tightly closed. Yet she could feel the burning warmth of his breath against her cheek. Every inch of her body was a captive of the muscled power of his. Each grasping breath of air she took inhaled deeper his potent male scent until she felt suffocated by it.

"Get away from me!" The words rushed in a desperate whisper through her clenched teeth. "I don't want you to touch me!"

"No?" His low voice laughed at her silently. "I ought to make love to you. It's what a hellcat like you deserves."

Her mind cried out in alarm, although not a sound escaped her lips. She had been so afraid for her life that she hadn't even considered the possibility that he might molest her. Lashes opening, her turquoise green eyes rounded with fear as she jerked her head to plead openly for him not to harm her.

The sudden action brought her lips against his mouth, warm and firm and as motionless as her own. Paralyzed by the unexpected contact, she could only lie there beneath him, unmoving and not daring to breathe. Any second she expected to feel the brutal possession of his kiss, and the thought burned like a fire through her veins.

"Please," she whispered when nothing happened. "Please let me go. I swear, I swear I won't tell the police."

The movement of her lips against his seemed to break the spell, but Brandy didn't know which direction he was going to take. A coiled tension seemed to take charge of him as his dark eyes raked her face.

In the struggles, his hat had come off. Brandy's eyes were drawn almost unwillingly to the dark, nearly black hair that grew thickly away from his forehead, its unkemptness like the rest of his appearance. A charged second went by before he replied.

"What won't you tell the police?" There was a watchful narrowing of his dark pupils as he moved a fraction of an inch away from her mouth.

"I ... I won't tell them I saw you," she promised shakily. "I mean ... I didn't actually see you stealing any cattle, so that would be the truth. I promise I won't say anything about meeting you."

His mouth thinned into a smile. "So you guessed why I'm out here?"

Hesitantly she nodded, wondering if she should have said nothing about rustling cattle. Maybe it would only make him more determined that she shouldn't get away.

With unbelievable swiftness for a man so large, he rolled away from her and on to his feet in one fluid movement. He towered above her prone figure, his hands lightly balanced on his hips.

"And you promise to keep my little secret?" he questioned with a definite undertone of mocking amusement.

"If you let me go," Brandy qualified the promise hastily.

Slowly she inched into a sitting position, afraid to take her eyes off the man watching her so intently. For the first time she noticed the rips in her blouse, the white material showing dots of red blood where the thorns must have scratched as well as torn her blouse. She tried her best to make certain she was still decently covered without drawing attention to her actions.

"If...if you could give me directions..." she faltered nervously.

"Where do you live?" he interrupted.

"At the Ames house—my father is Stewart Ames. It's only about fifteen miles east of Saguarro Ranch headquarters, up on the ridge," Brandy explained as quietly as she could, as the fear slowly lessened its grip on her throat.

He stood for a minute, then shook his head. "I'm afraid I'm not familiar with the place. I vaguely remember that there is a house on that graveled road, but just where it is from here I couldn't tell you. And I especially couldn't give you specific enough directions for you to make it in the dark."

Brandy believed him. She didn't know why exactly,

24

but something in his tone of voice said he was telling the truth. She scrambled to her feet, clutching the opening of her blouse together in one hand. Even standing in front of him, she still had to look up into his face.

"All I need is a general direction to take," she assured him quickly. "Once I'm in more familiar territory, I can find my own way home."

"Will your parents be looking for you?" The man refused to let her pleading blue-green eyes fall under the force of his piercing gaze.

This time she debated silently whether she should lie or tell him the truth: the truth had kept her safe thus far, she decided.

"I don't know for sure whether they are or not," she answered honestly, "they went out this evening. It all depends on whether they check to see if I'm home or not when they come back."

"In other words, they may not miss you until morning," he insisted on making her meaning clearer.

Brandy looked down at her feet. "That's right."

He seemed to consider her answer very thoroughly. "As much as I would like to be rid of you," he said finally, "I can't send you back into the desert to stumble around in the dark. Maybe you'd make it home and maybe not. With my luck, you'd fall and break a leg, then someone would backtrack you to my camp and I'd get blamed." He turned away from her toward the fire, rubbing the rough beard on his chin with his hand. "That kind of trouble I don't need!"

"But—" Brandy started to protest.

"No arguments." His hand was raised in a halting gesture. "You'll stay here for the night. Tomorrow I'll take you back."

"But I can't stay here with you." The denial was out before she could check it.

He glanced over his shoulder, a wolfish gleam appearing in his eyes. "What's the matter? Are you afraid to trust a cattle rustler?"

Brandy swallowed and clutched her blouse tighter together. "Should I trust you?" she asked with false boldness.

"The only thing we'll be sharing tonight is the warmth from this fire," he told her in no uncertain terms. "Of course, standing clear over there, you're not going to get much benefit from it."

Fear and her subsequent struggles had made Brandy impervious to the cool temperature of the desert night, but at his words, it penetrated the thin material of her blouse with shivering intensity. Suppressing a shudder, she walked to the promised warmth of the fire, keeping a couple of steps between herself and the man. Uncertain as to how far she could trust him, it was a cautious truce as she watched him with a wary eye.

The radiating heat from the small fire was blessedly welcome, and her lashes started to flutter down in silent gratitude when she saw the movement of the man's hand to his side. She stiffened at the sight of

26

the leather sheath attached to the man's belt and the knife that he removed from it. Again the firelight flashed menacingly off the steel blade and the old fear came racing back.

The man didn't seem to notice the hasty step Brandy took backward. "Are you hungry?" He moved to the opposite side of the fire from her, and knelt beside some sticks that made an improvised roasting spit.

"Yes," she admitted in a low voice as she saw the cooked animal skewered by the stick. Cutting off a portion of the meat, he handed it to her. Her fingers closed gingerly around the bone that jutted out of the cooked meat. "What is it?" she asked, lowering herself to a cross-legged position beside the fire.

"Jackrabbit." He didn't glance up as he sliced off another leg. "It probably will be a little tough, but it's food."

Biting into it, Brandy discovered that the meat was a little stringy, but she was too hungry to care. The bone was nearly cleaned before a thought occurred to her.

"Did you shoot this?" she asked.

"Yes," he nodded.

"One shot?"

Her persistence brought his curious gaze to her face. "Yes. Why?"

A faint smile curved her lips. "It was a rifle shot I heard around sundown that made my horse bolt and left me out here."

27

"So I'm to blame after all, is that what you're saying?" he said with challenging softness.

"No." She shook her head, honey-gold curls dancing briefly. "I was so busy watching the sunset that I didn't bother to ground-tie him. It was a foolish mistake."

"Yes," he agreed dryly.

Tearing off another chunk of rabbit meat, Brandy chewed it quietly and wished the man hadn't been so quick to agree. It wasn't as if she had been trying to blame him for driving off her horse, not even subconsciously. At least she had more right to be riding in this area of the desert than he did! He was nothing but a common thief.

CHAPTER TWO

WHEN THE RABBIT was eaten, the fruit of the prickly pear cactus was offered as dessert. With all the hunger pangs satisfied, Brandy sat beside the fire sipping hot, strong coffee from a tin cup. There was a desire to linger over the coffee, but since there was only one cup, she was sipping it hurriedly so the man could drink his.

"That was good," she murmured when she had drained the last of the black coffee from the cup and handed it back to him. "The whole meal was good. Of course, I was so hungry I don't think I would have cared what I ate."

The man simply nodded and filled the tin cup with more coffee.

Brandy tilted her head curiously to one side. "Do you eat this way often? I mean, taking food from the land?"

"Whenever I'm out on the desert," he admitted with an offhand shrug. "I don't like to be slowed up carrying supplies on a packhorse."

Yes, Brandy thought to herself, there were probably times when he had to travel fast to keep from being caught. It made sense to travel light.

"Are you out here often?"

He studied her across the fire for a long second.

"Often enough," was his noncommittal reply. He took a large swallow of coffee, not giving any indication that it was as scalding hot as Brandy remembered.

She started to probe further into his answer, then she realized that he had deliberately not been specific. The less she knew about his activities, the less she would be able to tell the authorities. Maybe he didn't trust her to keep the promise she had made not to say anything about seeing him. Actually she wasn't positive she would keep it; maybe he guessed that.

He took another swallow of coffee, then dumped the dregs on the porous ground. Brandy watched with sudden wariness as he rose to his feet and walked to the western saddle that was sitting several feet from the fire, barely within its circle of light. A pair of saddlebags were hooked over the saddle horn. Crouching beside it, he opened one flap and removed a white box.

Curiosity got the best of her. "What's that?" she asked when he straightened with the box in hand, and started to walk back to the fire.

"A first-aid kit," he answered an instant before she saw the familiar red cross emblem on the top. "It's time those scratches you have were cleaned."

Brandy glanced at her forearms and the vivid red marks drawn on her flesh by the thorns that had barely broken the skin. She had been conscious of them smarting now and then, but none of them were deep, not even those that had torn her blouse. They looked sore, but they really didn't bother her.

"They don't hurt," she murmured, unconsciously protesting against the need for any first aid to be administered. "I hardly feel them at all."

But he was already squatting on his heels beside her, the wide-brimmed hat pushed back on his head. The box was opened and he was pouring antiseptic from a plastic bottle on to a gauze pad.

"You'll feel them if infection sets in," he said firmly.

Logically Brandy knew he was right. There was no telling what germs were on those spiky thorns, yet she was uneasy about having him treat her.

"I'll do it," she said to him firmly, and reached out for the gauze.

"It's easier for me." His fingers closed over the hand she had extended and he began cleaning one long welt on that forearm.

The firelight fully illuminated his face: this was the first time that she had been able to study him at close quarters. There was a ruthless strength to his powerfully defined features that reinforced her first impression that he was dangerous. The dark brown, nearly black, of his beard, eyebrows, hair and eyes was intensified by the sun-brown shade of his skin. The half-grown beard concealed what she guessed would be a strongly defined jawline and angular, lean cheeks.

Without the beard, she thought he would look handsome in an intimidating kind of way. She decided that he was growing it for a disguise. There was something vaguely familiar about him, too, which was silly,

31

because she didn't know anyone who possessed that potent aura of masculinity.

The one thing about him that surprised her was his lack of a furtive air. He was so self-assured, so completely in command, not at all the way she expected a man to be who lived outside the law. Yet she wondered why with all that self-assurance and self-confidence, a man who had to be in his early to mid-thirties would become a cattle rustler. Admittedly, there was something of a throwback about him.

His attention had switched to her other arm where he was ministering to the cuts and scratches there. His hands and fingers were strong and brown, and did not bear any calluses of hard work. Surprisingly she discovered they were gentle, too.

With a start, she realized how lucky she had been to come off unharmed during the struggle she had had with him. He was very well muscled and could have broken a bone with little effort, or badly bruised her with a little more pressure applied. But he hadn't. The knowledge made her feel a bit safer in his company.

The last scratch on her arm was cleaned and disinfected. He tossed the gauze pad into the fire and reached for the box. The stinging sensation had left her skin.

"Thank you," she offered gratefully.

The sideways glance he gave her cocked a dark eyebrow. "Take off your blouse and I'll clean those scratches on your chest."

Brandy stared wide-eyed at him, noticing the fresh

gauze in his hand and the antiseptic bottle. Automatically her hand moved defensively to the collar of her blouse, and his mouth quirked in dry amusement at her action.

"We've been through the hellcat routine," he said patiently. "Do you really want to waste all that energy fighting again? Either you take the blouse off or I will." It was no idle threat.

Her breathing became shallow. "Give me the pad and I'll clean them myself," she stated.

"You would have to be a contortionist to see what you're doing. It will be faster and more thorough if I do it." A wicked glitter of amusement entered his eyes when Brandy mutely shook her head in refusal. "A woman's body doesn't embarrass me. Pretend I'm a doctor."

"But you're not," she muttered in a frustrated protest.

"You're only going to make it more embarrassing for yourself by making a production out of this," he reasoned. "Put aside your modesty."

Reluctantly she admitted the truth of his statement, but it didn't stop her fingers from trembling as she undid the buttons of her blouse.

There had been a time in her first years as a teenager when she had been terrified that because of her slender build she would end up with a pancake bustline, and she had been relieved when the rounded, full curves had arrived. Now she was unbearably conscious of them as she removed the thin blouse and

33

held it nervously on her lap. Her gaze became riveted on the stitching around the collar of his suede vest.

The cool dampness of the gauze pad touched the scratch on her collarbone. Brandy held herself as rigid as a statue, knowing the lacy bra exposed much more than it concealed.

"You said your last name was Ames. What's your first?" he asked quietly, moving to another welt near her shoulder.

For an instant, Brandy was on the brink of refusing to answer his question. Then she realized he was only making conversation to put her at ease.

"Brandy." Her voice broke slightly.

"Brandy?" His gaze slid to her face in verification before it returned to the scratch on her shoulder. "It's a pity you don't carry around a sample of your namesake. I think you could do with a shot of it right now."

"Yes," she said with a shaky smile of agreement. "Wh-what's your name?"

He hesitated for a split second. "Jim."

No last name, just Jim. She knew he was concealing the rest of his identity from her. It was even possible that Jim wasn't his first name; he might have made it up for her benefit.

"I have to slip your strap down, Brandy, to get at this one scratch," he warned.

His fingers were already sliding it off her shoulder before she could form any protest. Her quick glance downward saw the red mark that slashed across the swell of her breast. Although prepared for his impersonal touch, she still wasn't able to keep from inhaling sharply as his hand touched her.

His gaze flashed quickly to her face in concern. "Did I hurt you?"

"No," she denied quickly, and a swift rush of beet-red swept over her face.

His head bent again to his task, but the heat of embarrassment didn't ease. The sensation of intimacy was simply too strong for Brandy to be casually indifferent.

"How old are you?" the man who had identified himself as Jim asked.

"Twenty." Brandy glanced to his face with a slightly bewildered frown. "Why?"

A corner of his mouth twitched as he slid her strap back into place, a suggestion of laughter in the dark eyes that met hers. "You blush like a teenager," he murmured, "or a virgin."

New waves of scarlet flamed in her cheeks. She would have loved to deny his perceptive statement, but she had the uneasy feeling that he would know she was lying. Not that she hadn't done her share of necking and petting while on dates—she simply hadn't been sufficiently aroused or tempted to go all the way.

"You can put your blouse back on." While she had been mentally defending herself, he had completed cleaning the last scratch and was turning away.

Brandy quickly slipped on her blouse, fumbling momentarily with buttons. Out of the corner of her eye, she watched Jim rise and walk to replace the first aid kit in the saddlebag. When he turned back to the fire, she self-consciously edged closer to the flame.

"Tired?" he asked.

She glanced at her watch, surprised to see it was nearly midnight. "Yes," she admitted uncertainly.

From the shadow of his saddle he picked up a bedroll and untied it, spreading it over the flat ground near the fire. It was small, big enough for only one person, and Brandy swallowed tightly.

"You can sleep here," he instructed.

"Where are you going to sleep?" she asked quickly as he moved back toward the saddle.

He flashed her a laughing look, his gaze swerving from her face to the thin white blouse. "Since you've put your modesty back on, I don't think you're going to offer to share the blanket with me even if it gets cold." He reached down and picked up a heavy lined jacket. "So I guess I'll have to sleep by the fire."

"You can have the bedroll," Brandy stated, "I can stay here by the fire."

"Get in the bedroll and go to sleep." His thumb arched toward the blankets spread invitingly on the ground. There wasn't any laughter in this tone, only command.

Reluctantly she obeyed, resenting the fact that if she didn't, he would probably carry her there bodily if necessary. She gave him an angry glare as she walked by, to let him see that she didn't like to be ordered around. But he appeared indifferent to her.

36

While he added more fuel to the fire, Brandy tugged off her boots and slipped beneath the blanket, cradling her head on her arm. She didn't feel the least bit sleepy. As she gazed at the fire that had begun to crackle brightly, she wondered if her parents had noticed she wasn't in bed. This very minute they might be organizing a search party for her. Somehow she doubted that they would miss her before morning.

Her gaze shifted to Jim. With that bulky jacket on, he looked even bigger and stronger than before. What would her parents think if they met him?

A crazy question, since her own reactions had fluctuated so extremely. One minute she was terrified by him, in the next she was admiring his strength and assurance that made her feel so safe and secure. Then she was embarrassed by his cynical mockery, or bridling at the way he ordered her around as if she were a child and not an adult. The only certainty in her emotions was that she wasn't indifferent to him. No one could be for long.

Blinking tiredly, she wasn't aware of having fallen asleep. Her eyes focused bewilderedly on the yellow haze that filled the sky. Where were the stars? It couldn't be morning already. A twist of her head found the golden globe of the sun just peeping over the horizon.

Sighing, she snuggled deeper in the bedroll, her muscles and bones stiffly protesting at the night they had spent on the hard ground. The air still held the night's cold, biting at her nose and cheeks, and she rolled sleepily onto her side to face the campfire.

There were no flames. No heat was radiated from the circle of gray-white ashes. And there was no sign of Jim. Stunned, Brandy propped herself up on an elbow and looked to where the saddle had been last night. It was gone, too.

Had he left her? Had he decided not to risk being caught by helping her back home? Or had he sneaked away in the pre-dawn hours so he could be far away from this area in case she didn't keep her promise and told the authorities about him?

The wild flurry of questions raced unanswered through her mind, and throwing back the covers, she scrambled from the bedroll. She reached hastily for her boots. As she started to pull on the right one a horse snorted behind her.

"You'd better shake those boots out before you put them on." The low husky voice came from directly behind her. "A scorpion might have decided to use one for a nest during the night."

At the sound of his voice Brandy turned, a faint twinge of relief going through her at the sight of Jim's familiar figure leading the saddled horse toward the fire. He hadn't deserted her after all! Meeting the enigmatic darkness of his eyes, she found herself at a loss for words.

Turning back, she wisely shook the boot to be certain no creature had crawled inside before putting it on. "You should have got me up earlier," she accused briskly.

"You were sleeping, and there didn't seem to be any point in waking you up sooner than was necessary," he replied smoothly. "The coffee should still be warm enough to drink. Prickly pear fruit is the breakfast menu."

He tossed her the tin cup which she nearly didn't catch. "Coffee is good enough."

The small pot was sitting in the ashes. After pouring herself what was left in the pot, Brandy huddled near the campfire. Her thin blouse offered little protection against the cold, so she made use of what dying warmth remained in the ashes. Out of the corner of her eye she watched Jim tighten the saddle cinch on the liver-colored sorrel.

"Did you sleep well?" His question was unexpected.

"Yes, why?" Brandy cursed silently for sounding so defensive.

"Just wondered." His wide shoulders shrugged indifferently as the stirrup hung freely again along the horse's side.

He walked to the fire and dumped the coffee dregs from the pot on to the ashes. With a stick, he stirred the charred coals to be certain that no live ember remained.

"Did you think I'd left without you? Is that what's bothering you?"

Her gaze flew to his face, meeting his mocking and all too perceptive dark eyes. "You could have," she pointed out with an airy toss of her head.

"Yes, I could have." He straightened, the empty coffee pot in his hand. "Are you through with the cup?"

Brandy quickly swallowed the last of the now luke-warm liquid and handed him the cup, watching as he stowed the two items in the saddlebags. There only remained the bedroll to be put away. A shiver danced over her skin at the wished-for warmth of the blanket to be felt again.

"Come on, sun," she thought as she gazed at the yellow disc that had gained another notch in the morning sky. "Come and warm your desert!"

Standing in one place wasn't making her any warmer. She walked over to her bed and picked up the tightly-woven top blanket, and when she had shaken out the dust, Jim claimed it.

"I'll take it," he said.

Hesitating for a second, she finally released her hold on it with an inward shrug. Maybe he didn't think she was capable of rolling it up neatly enough to suit him.

Picking up the thinner groundsheet, she gave it a quick shake, and her side vision caught a metallic gleam. She turned curiously in time to see his knife-blade make a foot-long slash in the center of the blanket.

"What are you doing?" she frowned in astonishment.

The knife was replaced in the leather sheath that hung from his belt. "It's going to be an hour or more before it gets anywhere near warm. You'll have turned into an ice cube by then." Without further explanation the blanket, with its slit opening, was drawn over her head. "You can secure it around your waist with your belt."

For disbelieving seconds, Brandy stared at the blanket, now turned into a poncho. Already she could feel its warmth and the protection it offered against the cold.

Finally she raised her eyes to his face, and gently studied his expression. "You've ruined your blanket." A totally unnecessary observation, but she said it all the same.

"So I have," he agreed with a mocking twist of his male mouth.

To close the subject, he picked up the groundsheet Brandy had dropped. With a few expert flips he had it neatly in a compact roll. As he walked to the horse to tie the bundle behind the cantle, Brandy unbuckled her belt and drew it out of the loops of her denim jeans. She wanted to tell him how grateful she was, but she didn't know how to put it into words without sounding all gushy and artificial. And she sensed that he didn't require any spoken thanks.

Sighing, she secured the belt around the bulky folds of the blanket-poncho at her waist. She finished just as Jim completed smothering the ashen embers of the campfire. After a brief glance to make certain she was ready, he mounted his horse. Kicking his boot free of the left stirrup for Brandy to use, he grasped her forearm and helped her swing behind him on the horse.

"I know the general vicinity where your house should be," he said as she adjusted herself into as comfortable a position as was possible. "I imagine we'll meet up with a search party before we reach it."

Brandy agreed with him, balancing her hands on her thighs as Jim touched his heels to the horse's flanks. The sorrel started forward briskly, crossing their camp circle to head towards the north-east.

The gray ashes of the fire were covered with sand, and only their footprints gave evidence they had been there. Soon the desert would wipe away even that trace. Brandy found that thought to be sad—she wasn't exactly certain why.

Fresh and eager, the horse carried them effortlessly over the sandy ground, agilely skirting the thicker clumps of brush and cactus. The hush of the morning negated any need for conversation. The country around them was new to Brandy, although the far-reaching vistas were basically the same, viewed from a different angle.

Protected by the poncho and warmed by the body heat of the man riding in front of her, she found the ride to be an exhilarating way to start the day. The cool of the morning was the time that the desert wild-life came out to forage for food. It was a challenge to try to catch a glimpse of them before they scurried out of sight.

They had traveled a couple of miles before Brandy

noticed a change in the horse's gait. It had become less smooth as if offering resistance to the command of the reins. For a moment she thought the sorrel might have a rock lodged in his shoe. Tipping her head downward, she studied his stride for several feet, but couldn't see that he was favoring any hoof.

Glancing around Jim's shoulder, she saw the horse's ears pricked forward, his head held unnaturally high, tossing now and then as he champed to get control of the bit in his mouth. His gait remained joltingly stiff-legged.

"What's the matter with your horse?" Brandy leaned toward Jim's back to see the sternly tightlipped profile of her riding companion. "Has he suddenly decided he doesn't want us to ride double?"

"No," was the abrupt response.

But he must have agreed with Brandy that something was wrong, because at that moment he checked the horse to a halt. Still the muscular sorrel danced nervously in place, his neck arching higher. Brandy frowned and started to ask again what was wrong.

"Damn!" The softly muttered oath stopped her question.

At almost the same instant, a touch of the reins pivoted the horse on its haunches. Brandy had barely recovered her balance from that unexpected movement and the horse was bounding into a canter at a right angle to their former path. She had to clutch Jim's waist to stay on board.

They were obviously fleeing from something or

someone—Brandy didn't have time to look, but she guessed it was someone. It was either the search party looking for her or some kind of legal authorities possibly investigating a report of cattle rustling.

Just as Brandy adjusted to the leaping rhythm of the canter, the horse slid to a stop near a rocky outcrop. Her left arm tried to circle Jim's waist for support, but it was seized by his.

"Get down!" he ordered, nearly pushing her off the side before she could co-ordinate her body to obey the command.

She moved quickly out of the way of the dancing hooves, expecting the horse and rider to gallop away and leave her there. Instead Jim was off the horse a split-second after her. She watched in wide-eyed amazement as he held the reins of the nearly panic-stricken horse and unsaddled him at the same time. The saddle and pads were dropped carelessly on to the ground as he moved to the horse's head.

"What's wrong?" Brandy raked a confused hand through her amber-gold hair.

"Sandstorm," Jim answered tersely.

Something, not someone. Looking to the north, Brandy realized the dark haze on the horizon was not a distant mountain range but a rapidly moving sandstorm. Her stomach twisted itself into knots of fear.

She had witnessed the unbelievable fury of such storms before, but her view had always been from the shelter of a sturdy, man-made structure. Never had she actually been in one, exposed and unprotected.

Her gaze darted in alarm to the tall, broad-shouldered man wrestling with the plunging, rearing horse. She saw that he was fighting to unbuckle the bridle.

"You aren't turning him loose?" she breathed.

At that moment the jaw strap came free of the buckle and the horse was tearing its head out of the bridle. Loose, the sorrel bolted away at a flat-out run.

"He's desert born and raised and knows more about surviving out here than we do." The tightly worded explanation was given as Jim moved swiftly to retrieve the saddle and pads. "Get over to the rocks."

The hand between her shoulder-blades didn't wait for her to obey and she was pushed roughly towards the outcropping of rocks. Once there, he scanned the uninviting expanse of jagged rocks, then handed her the saddle pads.

"Put these pads over there where those rocks come together in a vee," Jim instructed.

She didn't need to be told to hurry. The feeling of urgency was all around her. Jim planned for the rocks to take the force of the driving wind. While she jammed the thick pads into the tapering ragged corner, he was shaking out the groundsheet.

Casting an anxious eye at the approaching storm, Brandy turned to tell Jim that she was done. He was already there, wrapping part of the groundsheet around her and pulling her down with him to a half-sitting position against their rock wall.

His arms were around her, cradling her against the solidness of his chest. The groundsheet he tucked the rest of the way around both of them and drew it over their heads. In the quiet darkness of the protective cocoon, Brandy was aware of his muscular body lying heavily against hers. There was no thought to the intimacy of their positions, their closeness that made both heartbeats sound as one. She was only conscious of the way he was shielding her from the coming storm.

With the suddenness of a striking rattler, it was on them. The howling wind seemed to try to suck them away from the shelter of the rock. Brandy's arm instinctively tightened around Jim's waist.

Fine dust penetrated, choking her nose and throat with its tiny grains. The blasting sand seemed to come from every direction, stinging bombardments of a thousand needles, and Brandy knew that Jim was taking the brunt of the punishment.

The roar was deafening. The air she breathed was stifling hot and laden with suffocating particles. She wanted to tear away the cover and gulp in clean, fresh air even though she knew the raging storm made it impossible.

"I ... I can't breath," she murmured in a gasping, choking voice, her face buried alongside the strong column of his throat.

Jim drew her more tightly into his arms. "Hang in there, honey," he whispered forcefully. "We're going to make it. Just hang in."

Brandy closed her mind to everything except the reassuring beat of his heart beneath her head and the indomitable strength that seemed to flow from the male body that enveloped her.

A minute later became as long as an hour. And the storm raged, its hammering din of sand never seeming to abate. The heat, the noise, the suffocating dust, all combined to make it an unending nightmare. When Jim tried to turn her face away from the filtering sheepskin collar of his jacket, she resisted and tried to bury her head deeper.

"Brandy," his fingers slid gently through her curling hair, "Brandy, it's all right. You can come out now." His voice was warm and gently mocking.

When she still refused to move, he pulled away and prized her arms loose from around his waist. Then the quietness struck her and she opened her eyes to the sunlight. The groundsheet had been thrown back, its dark color indistinguishable with the thick film of sand that covered it.

"I can't believe it," Brandy sighed, sinking back against the saddle pads, slowly breathing in the air.

Tiny particles of dust remained in the air, but considerably less now that the storm had passed. Jim was leaning against the wall beside her.

"Can't believe what?" He glanced down at her, his dark eyes gentle yet mocking.

"I didn't think it was ever going to end." Brandy smiled at the blue sky above their heads.

She rolled her head to the side, lazily directing her

smile to him. A dark light entered his eyes, mysterious and compelling. A finger reached out to touch the turned-up tip of her nose, then trailed a dusty path down her cheek. Something in his touch made her heart skip crazily.

"Your skin feels like sandpaper." His mouth quirked.

The gritty film was everywhere. "You should see your whiskers!" she told him with a breathless laugh.

He grinned lazily, his hand leaving her cheek as he pushed himself to his feet. Upright, he extended his hand to her to help her to her feet. Without hesitation, she placed her hands in his firm grip and was pulled easily to her feet.

Her hand was still warmly held by his, not that Brandy minded. The chest that she had been so protectively locked against only minutes before was only inches away. She tipped her head to one side.

"Do you know," she said in a voice that was partly teasing and partly serious, "I haven't thanked you for all you've done? Last night and now?"

"I should claim my reward for rescuing you, shouldn't I?" Jim mocked huskily, the dark glitter of his eyes moving to her mouth.

They had been through too much together in less than twenty-four hours for Brandy to feel self-conscious. She raised herself up on tiptoes as Jim's hand cupped the back of her neck. Her fingers spread across his chest to balance herself.

With brown lashes fluttering down, she felt the

rough brush of his whiskers first, then the warmness of his mouth closing over hers. The kiss was gently firm, nothing tentative or uncertain about it, just like the man who gave it.

When the kiss came to an end, Brandy blinked in wonder of the utter disappointment she felt that it was over. She gazed into his eyes, veiled by sooty lashes, their expression unreadable. The hand at the back of her neck slowly tightened, drawing her to him.

She didn't need the pressure of his hand to tip her head back to receive his kiss. The hard demand of his mouth ignited a wildfire that spread swiftly to her veins, melting her limbs to pliant pieces of molding clay. Expertly he shaped her malleable body to the muscular contours of his.

Whirling in a mindless world ruled only by sensations, Brandy felt them exploding around her. Her pulse hammered like a mad thing in her ears. The inescapable gritty taste of sand was on her lips that had parted under the unresistible command of his. The heady male scent of him enveloped her like the drugging scent of burning incense. Nearly every inch of her skin felt the imprint of his masculine body.

Then the passion-arousing kiss was ended, and his mouth moved in reluctant slowness away from hers. Unconsciously Brandy sighed her regret, letting her head dip to resting position against his chest while she re-orientated her jumbled senses.

There was in impersonal gentleness in the hands that held her shoulders. It was echoed by the distantly

49

affectionate kiss he bestowed on the top of her head.

Puzzled by his obvious withdrawal, she tipped her head back to gaze into his impassive face. He used her motion away from him to release her completely.

"It would have been wiser if I hadn't done that," he murmured with a wry, self-derisive arch of his eyebrow as he turned away.

Brandy frowned, then laughed her confusion. "Why should you be sorry you kissed me? I'm not!"

Without glancing at her, Jim retrieved the saddle pads and laid them over the saddle. "Things have gone beyond the point where they can be easily explained," he answered cryptically. "That is my fault. But let's just say that I think it's best that we forget what happened a minute ago."

"Why?" she persisted.

"I don't want you to get the wrong idea." He gave the groundsheet an indifferent shake and draped it across the saddle, too.

It seemed as if she was lost in a maze and all his answers were leading her deeper into it, instead of a safe passage out.

"People kiss all the time. It's a very common practice between two people who find each other attractive," she reasoned with a confused shake of her head. "I may look young, but I'm not some blindly romantic teenager who's going to misinterpret a kiss as a declaration of love."

"You do look young and impressionable," Jim admitted with a faint twinkle in his eyes.

Anger burst suddenly inside her and she retorted scathingly, "Probably viewed from your advanced years, I do!" Immediately she was sorry she had lashed out at him when she had no cause. "I didn't mean to lose my temper," she apologized, but he was already smiling at her previous comment. "It's just that I don't understand what there is to regret in a kiss."

"I like you, Brandy. If I had known the type of person you were when you stumbled into my camp last night, all this talk now wouldn't be necessary."

Brandy sighed at the near helplessness of the conversation. "What's that supposed to mean, Jim?"

He studied her for a long moment before answering patiently. "There are quite a few things about me that you don't know, but I do."

Frustrated by his deliberately obscure answers, she turned away, lifting her hand in a helpless gesture. "I suppose you're married with three kids. Is that supposed to shock me or make me feel like a home-wrecker?"

A throaty chuckle rumbled mockingly. "I'm not married," he declared, with no attempt to conceal the amusement in his voice. He reached down and looped the canteen strap over his shoulder. "Come on, Brandy. We've got a long walk ahead of us."

For a few minutes Brandy had completely forgotten her predicament. Now she thought of her parents who were probably waiting anxiously for some word that she was all right. And here she was arguing with a cattle rustler who was being deliberately mysterious.

Taking a step forward to fall in beside him, she noticed his saddle and gear sitting on the ground. "Are you leaving your things behind?" she frowned.

"I can pick them up later."

Brandy supposed it would be foolish for him to carry the saddle over the same ground twice, considering how heavy it was. His long strides put Jim in the lead, although he did slacken his pace so that she could keep up.

Gazing over the vast expanse of rolling desert, dotted with shrubs and cactus, she was aware of the enormous size of it. A person could see for miles, yet there was nothing to be seen. "How are you ever going to find your horse?" She hurried to draw level with Jim as she asked the question.

"He'll probably head for the corral and water now that the storm is over," he replied.

The corral; Brandy guessed that was probably where he was holding the cattle he had stolen until his partners came to ship them out. She wondered if it was anywhere near the place that he had camped last night. Thinking back, she knew she had not heard any sound of cattle lowing close by. There had only been the rustle of the horse.

Covertly she studied his boldly chiseled profile. Curiosity returned as she tried to fathom his confusing answers of a few minutes ago. It was hopeless. Then she began wondering why a man who seemed capable of doing anything he wanted had chosen to be a cattle thief. It seemed such a shame.

"Jim?" Hesitantly she formed her question, the uneven ground beneath her feet demanding part of her attention. "Have you always stolen cattle? I mean, haven't you ever wanted to do something else?"

"I wondered how long it would take." He gave her an amused look.

"What?" she asked with a disgruntled sigh. He had avoided her question again with another ambiguous answer.

"I was talking about the female instinct to reform a man. Yours has finally surfaced." There was a definite sparkle of laughter in the dark eyes as the corners of his mouth deepened with suppressed amusement. "Were you going to give me a lecture in the error of my wicked ways?"

"I was just curious," she retorted defensively.

Although she waited for him to reply to her question, she waited in vain. Surrendering to the inevitable, she didn't bother to ask again.

CHAPTER THREE

THEIR WEAVING, twisting trail through the cactus and sage-studded desert had taken them over two miles of ground. As the crow flies, they had only covered about a mile and a half. The sun was well up in the sky and no coolness from the night remained. Jim had removed his jacket and unbuttoned his vest, while Brandy had removed the belt so that the poncho hung free and rebuckled it through the waist loops of her denims.

Halfway up the rock-strewn wall of a drywash, Brandy stopped to catch her breath. The honey-gold hair around her forehead had curled into damp ringlets from perspiration. At the top of the wash, Jim reached down to give her a hand up.

"You can rest up here," he insisted when she started to ignore his hand.

With a shrug of resignation she grabbed hold of his hand and scrambled with his help to the slanted rim of the wash. There she sat down, leaning back on one elbow in the scant shade of a palo verde.

"You can tell I'm used to riding and not walking," Brandy murmured with a self-deprecating smile.

"This sun can drain the energy out of anyone." He opened the canteen and handed it to her.

The water was brackishly warm, but the liquid still

soothed her dry throat. Taking another long drink, she handed it back to him. There was a whirring sound in her ears that she attributed to the heat and exhaustion of their trek through the desert; then it seemed to grow louder.

"Jim, I think I hear a helicopter." The minute she voiced the comment, Brandy became more positive that she was right. Shading her eyes against the glare of the sun, she searched the sky where she thought the sound was coming from. Sunlight flashed on a metallic object flying comparatively low to the ground. "There it is!" she pointed.

Turning, she saw that Jim was watching it, too, the brim of his dust-covered hat shading out the sun. His gaze had narrowed. It remained that way as it swung to her in a piercing regard.

"It's a search party," he said in unnecessary explanation.

The relief left her voice. "I know."

That meant that in a few short minutes she would be rescued and winging home to the welcoming arms of her parents. But if Jim was seen—Brandy knew she couldn't bear to see him arrested for stealing cattle, not after all he had done for her. He was a criminal, and liking him didn't change that. Regardless of whether it was wrong or not, she knew she had to help him get away.

"They haven't seen us yet." Her anxious turquoise eyes scanned his impassive features. "You can hide in that clump of mesquite over there. They'll never even

55

know you were here, Jim, if you hide right now."

"You're not going to turn me in?" He smiled crookedly at her.

"I can't." She glanced over her shoulder at the slow-flying helicopter that was drawing steadily nearer their position on the rim of the drywash. "They're getting closer. Hurry, Jim, before they see you!"

As he slowly rose to his feet, she scrambled upright with him. The lazy smile was still making a curve in his beard as she gazed up at him. How she hated saying goodbye!

"Take care of yourself," she whispered tightly.

He hestiated, his expression growing serious. "I'm not going anywhere, Brandy."

"But—" She looked anxiously over her shoulder.

The helicopter was close enough for her to make out the pilot and the man sitting beside him. Even as she realized that, she saw the pilot point toward them. It was too late.

"Oh, Jim!" Bitter tears filled her eyes. "They've seen us. They've seen you."

Reaching out, he brushed an imaginary lock of hair behind her ears. "Brandy, I'm sorry. I am very sorry," he murmured cryptically.

"I'm the one who's sorry," she insisted with a confused frown.

His hand settled over her shoulder, turning her round. "There's a clearing over there where the helicopter will probably land to pick us up."

With Jim more or less pushing her along ahead of

him, they started toward the clearing. Brandy couldn't believe it was all happening.

"Aren't you going to try to get away?" she accused in disbelief. "You still might make it." Jim didn't answer, but kept pushing her toward their destination. "Do you want to get caught, is that it? You'll go to jail." The helicopter was very near and she had to shout the last to make herself heard above its din.

Not until they had reached the clearing did he speak, his hand falling away from her shoulder as he suddenly seemed very remote. "I'm not a cattle rustler, Brandy." His voice was controlled and clear.

"But you said—" she started to protest.

"No, you said it," he corrected smoothly.

He seemed so completely different somehow. She made a frowning study of him, trying to figure out what it was. She tipped her head warily to one side.

"Who are you, anyway?" she demanded.

Dust swirled around them as the helicopter descended on to the clearing. Its arrival distracted Brandy as she turned to face it, shielding her eyes against the grains of sand kicked up by the propeller blades that whirled on top. The pilot remained at the controls as the second man stepped out and ran in a crouching position toward Brandy and Jim.

A wide grin of relief was splitting the man's face. "Dammit, Jim," he exclaimed as he reached them, vigorously shaking Jim's hand, "am I glad to see you're all right! Raymond saw your horse heading for the main house just before the storm hit." Then the man glanced at Brandy. "You must be the Ames girl."

Numbly she moved her head in an affirmative nod as the poncho-blanket flapped roughly against her side from the whirling wind generated by the spinning helicopter blades. Her confusion was increasing with each ticking second. Her mind raced to separate the true facts from the false. The man appeared to know Jim very well, and Jim *was* his name. In her bewilderment, Brandy recognized that he had been more concerned about finding Jim safe than her. Jim wasn't a cattle rustler, he was somebody important, but who?

Then Brandy remembered that initial sensation that there was something about him that was familiar. With eyes narrowed against blowing dust, she turned to study his face. His features were obscured by the beard and the wide brim of his hat pulled low on his forehead. Obsidian-dark eyes were returning her gaze with cool alertness.

"Are you ready?" he asked. Part of her mind registered the fact that Jim was repeating the question put forth by the other man, but she stared without answering, trying desperately to recognize him. "Miss Ames, are you ready to leave?"

Miss Ames! The formal term of address jolted Brandy out of her daze. If it had been issued in gentle mockery instead of such distant politeness, she might not have felt quite so shocked. It had always been just Brandy and Jim.

"Yes." She nodded her head in accompaniment of

the softly-spoken agreement that was whipped away unheard by the noisy chop of the helicopter.

It was the other man's hand, not Jim's, that took a guiding hold of her arm and led her in a crouching walk to the open sides of the helicopter. The man helped her into the far rear seat, gesturing toward the seat belts to strap herself in.

Feeling strangely betrayed, Brandy wouldn't allow herself to look at Jim as he climbed effortlessly into the seat beside her. While the other man took the seat beside the pilot, she concentrated on buckling her seat belt tightly.

The man leaned sideways to shout above the deafening roar of the motor to the pilot. "Did you radio the sheriff that we found the Ames girl with Corbett?"

The pilot nodded affirmatively and the upward motion of the helicopter began.

Corbett! The name struck Brandy like a blow to the stomach. The image flashed in her mind of a dark-haired, dark-eyed man with bluntly carved cheek and jaw, the strong chin with its faint cleft. Sardonic grooves were etched either side of a cynical yet blatantly sensual male mouth. The rest of the image she recognized, the dark eyes that could glitter with cold menace or sparkle with mockery or be totally veiled so that no emotion at all was revealed.

The beard and the circumstances had kept her from guessing his identity. Who would ever have guessed, she reasoned in silent desperation, that a disreputable-looking cowboy camped alone in the desert would turn out to be James Corbett the actor?

Shock waves of recognition quaked her shoulders as she admitted who he really was. She felt sick to her stomach. How he must have laughed at her! He had probably thought it was hilariously funny that she had mistaken him for a cattle rustler. She could imagine him relating the tale for the amusement of his acting friends. What a fool she had made of herself!

Flames of supreme embarrassment burned her cheeks. She sank her teeth into her lower lip to hold back the sob of injured pride that would make her humiliation complete.

Through the veil of her lashes, her traitorously bright blue-green eyes darted a look of smoldering resentment at the man seated beside her. His dark eyes met the look emotionlessly before he diverted their attention to the desert scrub the helicopter was flying above.

Brandy jerked her head to the front, riveting her gaze on the pilot. Jim must have realized that she had finally recognized him, and now that his little game was over, he no longer found her amusing. With a little catch of her breath, she discovered that she still thought of him as Jim. Starting now, she had better begin thinking of him as James Corbett, celebrity and actor.

The pilot pressed the earphone of his headset more tightly against his ear, then signaled to the man in the co-pilot's seat to pick up the set of earphones hooked on the lower part of the control panel. Adjusting it over his head, the man spoke into the microphone mouthpiece, then listened.

Grimacingly wryly at the pilot, the man turned in his seat toward Jim. "There are reporters at the Ames house," he shouted. "Somehow they heard the search party had been instructed to look for you, too. Do you want to land at Saguarro instead?"

The swift glance Brandy darted at Jim encountered his measuring look. His mouth was compressed into a grim line of displeasure. She wanted only to go home and bring this miserable nightmare to an end, but it seemed she was going to have to run through a gauntlet of reporters before she reached the sanctuary.

"We'll go to the Ames house," was the terse command.

The man moved his shoulders in a shrug that said Jim was the boss and relayed the message to the pilot. Within a few minutes, Brandy saw the familiar buildings of her home just ahead. Cars, trucks and horse trailers littered the driveway and the area around the stable.

As the helicopter began its downward descent, using the graveled road in front of her house for its landing pad, a group of people surged forward to meet it. Brandy caught a glimpse of the anxious faces of her parents in the crowd before they were lost in the cloud of dust churned up by the rotating blades.

When it had settled to the ground, Jim ordered the pilot to turn the motor off. Its sputtering stop left the slowing, centrifugal whirl of the blades to fill its silence. Fumbling with her belt, Brandy finally got it unbuckled and started to crawl out of the helicopter.

Jim waited for her on the ground, but she ignored the large hand that offered to help her and jumped down unassisted. His broad chest blocked her path to the crowd: unwillingly, she let her gaze be drawn to his face. She was more wary of him now than she had ever been before.

"Excuse me, Mr. Corbett." Her voice sounded cool and surprisingly self-possessed. She didn't want to hear whatever it was that he had been on the point of saying. "My parents are waiting for me."

Brushing past him, she hurried to the smiling, relieved faces that belonged to her parents. The smile she gave them was forced and taut as she tried to guess what they were thinking about their daughter's return in the company of a celebrity.

Lenora, her mother, looked calm and happy. The camel tan trouser suit that she wore was subtly tailored to reveal her slender figure. Her medium-length hair was ash-blonde, cunningly streaked with gray to give her a sophisticated yet intellectual appearance. It was in her mother's arms that Brandy first sought shelter.

"You gave us such a scare, darling," Lenora Ames scolded as she cupped her daughter's face in her hands and laughed in relief. "You look like a grubby little urchin."

Brandy realized that she probably did look a sight in

her dust-encrusted poncho and the gritty fine sand that clung to her hair, skin, and clothes.

"I am a mess," she agreed before turning to her father's burly figure.

She had taken only one step toward him before she was enveloped in his hearty bear-hug. His dark, curling hair was peppered with gray, but his sun-burned face was still youthfully handsome.

"Are you all right, Brandywine?" Stewart Ames whispered in her ear, using his own pet name for her.

"I'm fine, Daddy." She hugged him a little tighter. Over his shoulder, she could see the reporters clustering around Jim Corbett. Cameras were clicking pictures, and she knew several had been taken of her reunion with her parents.

When her father released her from his embrace, it seemed to be a signal for the reporters to close in. There were only three, but the questions bombarded her as if they came from double that number.

"How do you feel, Miss Ames?"

"Fine," she nodded.

"Is it good to be home?"

"Of course."

"How did you get lost?"

"What was it like spending a night on the desert?"

"Tell us about it?"

The questions followed one another in such rapid succession that Brandy had barely focused her thoughts on one than another was thrown at her. Bewilderedly trying to decide which question to answer

63

first, she didn't notice Jim's approach. Suddenly he was there, smoothly introducing himself to her parents, and Brandy felt very proud of the way they reacted to him. They were respectful without being awed at his status.

"We heard you were caught in the sandstorm, Mr. Corbett," her father commented.

"Miss Ames," one of the reporters broke in, "what did you do when the sandstorm came up?"

There was a pause that allowed Brandy to answer. "Actually J ... Mr. Corbett saw the storm approaching and we were able to find shelter in some rocks until it blew over," she explained, hurriedly correcting the instinct to use his first name.

"Do you mean you and Mr. Corbett were together when the sandstorm hit?" a second reporter queried.

"I—that is—" Stammering, Brandy realized too late that no one had been told that she and Jim had been together prior to their rescue. Her eyes wildly sought assistance from Jim. There was no one else who could help.

"Miss Ames and I met last night," he announced calmly to the now intensely curious reporters, "she had lost her way in the dark, saw the fire from my camp and came in."

He made it sound so matter-of-fact, as if it was the most natural thing in the world, and not something that would cause comment.

"Then the two of you spent the night together on the desert, is that right?"

Jim Corbett smiled coldly. "I guess you would have to put it that way, yes."

"Where did you get those scratches on your arm, Miss Ames?"

Brandy glanced almost with surprise at the marks on her arms. She had completely forgotten about them. She wished she had remembered them and hidden them from beneath her poncho. Thank heaven the poncho covered her ripped blouse! That would really raise some eyebrows.

"Cactus and mesquite thorns," she answered, "I ran into some cactus and mesquite thorns."

"What were you running from?" one reporter laughed rather snidely.

She crimsoned, remembering her mad flight into the desert when she had seen the knife in Jim's hand. She could not possibly tell them that.

"Are you asking Miss Ames if I chased her around the campfire?" There was a mocking lift of one eyebrow at the reporter. "I think she was using a figure of speech when she said "ran into" some cactus and mesquite thorns."

"That's right," she agreed quickly.

"Why don't you describe for us what it's like to be stranded in the desert with James Corbett?" A reporter teased Brandy with a suggestive wink.

She waited, half expecting Jim to speak up to reveal that she hadn't known who he was. But he said nothing, leaving her to parry the question as best she could.

65

"To be honest," she said hesitantly, "by the time I saw the fire last night I was so grateful there was another human being around that I didn't care who it was."

"But afterward?" the reporter prompted.

"Afterward—" Brandy faltered again.

Jim picked up the sentence where she left off. "—she ate some of the rabbit I cooked. I put some antiseptic on her scratches and she went to sleep beside the fire. It wouldn't make a very good movie script, would it?"

Not the way he put it, Brandy thought to herself as the others laughed a little self-consciously. He had deliberately omitted the damaging parts, like the humiliating way she had thought he was a cattle thief and the fact that her scratches were not limited to her arms. She sent up a silent prayer of gratitude that he had, because she never would have been able to endure the tongue-wagging that would have followed the publication of those items.

"Mr. Corbett has quite a reputation with the ladies. Were you concerned about spending the night with him, Miss Ames?"

"I never even thought about his reputation," Brandy answered honestly, since she hadn't known who he was.

Even now she couldn't admit to knowing anything about him personally, but a man as ruggedly masculine and virile as he was, and a celebrity too, probably had had a long string of beautiful women in his life.

Something inside her froze a little at that thought, remembering that expert kiss he had given her, and the open way she had responded.

She had been so stupidly naïve. No wonder he had felt the need to tell her that the kiss meant nothing! He was a star and she was a nobody, and a not very glamorous nobody, too.

"Lost the way you were, it must have been quite thrilling to be found by James Corbett," one reporter observed.

Humiliating was the word, Brandy corrected him silently as she glanced at Jim with an upward sweep of the lashes. His dark eyes were glittering at her with that mocking light so reminiscent of the night before. Then she noticed the cynical twist of his mouth and turned away.

"Yes, it was," she lied calmly.

"Miss Ames—" the question forming on another reporter's lips never was completed.

"Fellers, fellers!" The man who had been in the helicopter with them stepped into the circle of people, a good-natured but firmly commanding expression on his face. "I think that's enough questions, don't you? I'm sure Miss Ames is tired and thirsty and much in need of a relaxing few hours in the comfort of her home after all she's been through. And I know Mr. Corbett is going to want to rest up before we start filming tomorrow morning. You have your stories, so let's break this gathering up."

Although they grumbled, none of the reporters

protested too earnestly to the request. As they began to disperse, Brandy realized that she wasn't going to be able to enter her home without saying some form of goodbye. Drawing on the composure of her parents who had steadfastly remained at her side during all the questioning, she turned to Jim.

"Goodbye, Mr. Corbett," she said stiffly. "I appreciated your help."

His mouth tightened for a second as if in irritation. She supposed it was because she hadn't sounded sufficiently impressed that she had had the privilege of spending so much time in his company. Then he challengingly offered his hand in goodbye, and she had to resist the impulse to slap it away.

"It's been a pleasure meeting you, Miss Ames," he murmured.

Her hand rested limply in his, not responding to the firm clasp of his fingers.

"I'm sure you found it amusing." Brandy smiled coldly as she made the sweetly cutting comment.

His grip tightened with painful pressure when she tried to slip her hand away. There was a swift narrowing of his dark eyes as he made a thorough study of her coolly polite expression. Then his gaze darted to the reporters, still lingering near their cars.

"You will be explaining that remark." The threatening promise was issued in an ominously soft tone meant only for Brandy to hear. Her hand was released as he nodded politely to her parents and pivoted toward the waiting helicopter.

For a few seconds, Brandy watched him striding away before she turned to her parents. Her mother curved a comforting arm around her waist and started toward the house.

"You go on in," Stewart Ames instructed. "I'll be there in a few minutes. I want to thank the men again for all they've done."

Inside the house, the tension that Brandy hadn't been aware of slipped away like the shedding of a coat. The muscles in her legs ached from her long walk over the rocky desert, she was tired from her night spent on the ground, and she felt caked with perspiration and grime.

"You must be hungry," her mother smiled, her green eyes still bright with relief at Brandy's safe return. "I'll fix you some soup and sandwiches." Then she laughed. "I'd better fix some for all of us. I just realized Stewart and I haven't even had breakfast. I'd just poured the orange juice when he discovered you weren't in your room and your bed hadn't been slept in."

That confirmed what Brandy had suspected. She almost wished they had discovered she was gone the night before; maybe she would have been found before she stumbled into Jim's camp. In all probability, though, she wouldn't have been and her parents would have spent endless hours imagining all sorts of terrible things.

"I didn't think you would miss me before morning," she admitted with a tired sigh. She knew her parents would want a more explicit account of what had happened than the carefully worded details she had given the reporters, and at this moment, she didn't feel up to it. "Look, Mom, what I really want right now is a long, hot bath," she said, changing the subject while she still could "Why don't you go ahead and fix us something to eat and it'll be ready when I get out of the tub."

AN HOUR LATER, she entered the spacious kitchen of coral and white where the tantilizing smell of hot tomato soup made her stomach growl. Her freshly-washed hair curled damply about her head, droplets of water dotting the shoulders of her clean, blue-striped blouse. Revitalized by the bath, she sniffed appreciatively at the soup on the stove and sent her parents a sunny smile.

"What happened to that little girl that looked like a desert rat?" her father teased, rising from the chair at the table to hold one out for Brandy.

"She got washed down the drain," she declared.

With the ordeal over, the appetites of all three had returned. Not until that had been partially satisfied did her parents' curiosity surface and Brandy was faced with relating what really happened.

"A cattle rustler," Stewart Ames chuckled softly when she haltingly explained her failure to recognize Jim Corbett. "That really must have been a blow to his ego!"

"Well, he certainly paid me back," retorted

Brandy. "It was unforgivable of him to let me go on thinking he was a cattle thief. He should have told me who he was. When I think of the way he was laughing at me behind my back—" She attacked the crackers in her soup, leaving the sentence unfinished. "It's humiliating!"

"You must admit there's an amusing side of it, Brandy," her mother chided the indignant outburst. "And it might have been awkward, even embarrassing, for Mr. Corbett to tell you who he was."

"Nothing could embarrass that man!" she snapped, then realized that it wasn't fair to answer so sharply. None of this had been her parents' fault and she shouldn't be taking her wounded pride out on them. "Can we change the subject? I don't want to talk about James Corbett any more."

Those were famous last words, as she learned to her chagrin the next morning when she arrived at the arts and crafts shop to go to work. She had barely stepped inside the rear door when she was accosted by her wide-eyed, carrot-topped girl friend, excitedly waving the morning paper.

"Brandy, is this true?" Karen Justin demanded in a gleeful voice. "Did James Corbett really find you wandering around in the desert, lost and frightened? James Corbett, the movie star?"

Brandy turned away to hang up her jacket on the employees' rack in the back room, fighting the waves of frustration that swamped her.

"Actually I found him," she answered in a tautly

71

controlled voice. "Is the coffee done?" The first one to arrive at the shop in the morning always put the coffee pot on so that there would be time for a shared cup before they unlocked the doors.

"Yes, I think so," Karen shrugged indifferently, and reverted back to her original topic. "You've got to tell me everything that happened!"

Brandy's lips thinned with exasperation as she filled a mug with hot coffee from the pot. "It's all in the papers. You can read it for yourself," she said with determined disinterest, turning toward her friend.

Karen's brown eyes twinkled brightly. "Not all of it is in the papers, I'll bet. Come on, Brandy," she cajoled, "you can tell me everything. I won't tell a soul, I promise."

"I was out riding; my horse bolted; I started walking home and got lost in the dark. Then I stumbled into his camp, spent the night, started for home in the morning, got caught in the sandstorm, and the helicopter rescued both of us after that. And that's it," Brandy declared with an upward motion of her open palm.

There was a denying shake of Karen's flame-colored hair. "But what did you think when you realized he was James Corbett?"

"I was shocked." Brandy smiled bitterly at the memory of that moment. She sipped at the coffee. "Where's Mrs. Phillips?" she asked, referring to the owner of the shop.

"At the bank, and quit trying to change the

subject," was the scolding answer. "Now tell me, what all did you think about? Did he tell you about the movie he's starring in, the one they're filming out at Old Tucson?"

"No." Brandy picked at the hem of her cream-colored smock, the front richly embroidered with orange, yellow and blue intertwining flowers.

"Well, what did you talk about?" Karen asked after waiting and not receiving a more explanatory answer.

"Nothing in particular." Frowning, Brandy smoothed the hem over the blue of her cotton slacks.

Karen tipped her head to the side, the expression in her brown eyes becoming thoughtful. "There's something you aren't telling me, isn't there?" Her friend was much too perceptive. "You were alone in the desert with him, sitting around a campfire with a skyful of stars overhead. He made a pass at you, didn't he?"

"Don't be ridiculous!" Brandy denied forcefully.

But Karen saw the cherry-red dots that rosed on her cheeks. Breathing in sharply, she gasped, "He *did* kiss you! Oh, Brandy," Karen giggled, "James Corbett kissed you!"

That incident Brandy had not related to her parents. It was the one thing she was most anxious to forget about her weekend episode.

"It's not the way you're thinking at all," she denied self-consciously. "It was really quite innocent. Why, at the time I didn't even know who he—" She closed her mouth abruptly.

73

Karen stared at her bewilderedly. "You didn't know what?" she asked curiously. "You didn't know who he—was?" She completed the sentence with a question mark in her voice, a sandy red brow arching in disbelief at the seemingly only logical verb that could be inserted. "Is that what you meant?"

With an impatient, frustrated motion, Brandy set her coffee cup on the small utility table. "Yes, that's what I meant," she admitted grudgingly. "I didn't recognize him."

"You didn't recognize James Corbett!" Even though she had guessed the fact a second ago, Karen still didn't believe it when she heard Brandy confirm it. She sank on to the seat of a tall stool near the utility table. "You aren't serious?"

The newspaper had slipped from her hands on to her lap, opened to the page where the story of Brandy, and James Corbett's rescue was printed.

"Look at that picture of him." Brandy pointed defensively to the grainy newspaper photograph taken of the two of them being interviewed by the reporters. "Who would recognize him in that beard? Besides, the last person you're going to expect to meet camped out on the desert is a movie star!"

"What was he doing out there anyway?" her friend asked, momentarily sidetracked.

"I don't know," Brandy shrugged in irritation. "I heard him tell the reporters that he was looking for some peace and quiet."

Karen hugged her arms about her middle. "What

74

was it like to be kissed by James Corbett, Brandy?''

A sharp pain knifed into Brandy's heart. Even now, hurt by the way Jim had made her the object of fun, she found the vivid memory of his kiss very pleasant. She was vaguely ashamed to admit how much she had enjoyed it. A girl had her pride.

"Since I didn't know he was James Corbett when he kissed me, I didn't take notes. If I'd known, maybe I could have checked to see if there was any acceleration in my heartbeat or if my temperature rose," she retorted churlishly.

"You don't have to bite my head off." Karen recoiled slightly, startled by the sarcasm coming from Brandy, who was usually so easy-going and good-natured.

"I didn't mean to," she apologized with a tired sigh. "It's just that I'd like to put the whole incident out of my mind. It isn't very much fun to remember how he must have secretly laughed at my ignorance when I didn't recognize him." She glanced at her wristwatch, adjusting the leather sportsband around her wrist. "It's nearly nine. Did Mrs. Phillips leave the front door key on her desk?"

"I think so," Karen nodded, following as Brandy walked to their employer's office. "Are you going to see him again?"

Brandy stopped and frowned over her shoulder. "See him again? What do you mean?"

"Did he ask you out?"

"Of course not," Brandy laughed, but the sound

75

had a hollow ring. "You see too many movies, Karen."

"You don't see enough. Stranger things have happened in real life than what's shown on the movie screen, you know," the redhead declared with an airy toss of her head.

"Well, he didn't ask me out and it's quite improbable that he will," Brandy stated firmly. "If he did, I wouldn't accept."

"You wouldn't!" Karen repeated incredulously.

"He's already had enough laughs at my expense. Compared to someone with his experience I'm just a country girl. Sophisticated glamor girls, like his leading ladies, are definitely more his type anyway."

"Maybe he wants a change of diet," Karen suggested with an impish smile.

"Then he can find someone else. I don't care to see him again." Or at least, that was what she kept telling herself.

CHAPTER FOUR

THE SUN GLEAMED through the window on Brandy's honey-bright hair as she bent to sniff the gentle fragrance of the roses. The bouquet of long-stemmed red roses had been waiting for her when she came home from work that day.

Her first inclination had been to throw them away even before she had read the card that came with them. It was a childish reaction, but Brandy had been hounded all day by friends and strangers wanting to hear the "inside" story about her night on the desert with James Corbett.

Finally she had stopped protesting when they declared what a thrilling adventure it had been and let them think what they liked. Nothing she said ever seemed to change their minds.

After second thoughts, she had decided it would be wrong to throw away such beautiful flowers simply because she felt frustrated and unable to cope with the situation and the subsequent notoriety.

The message on the card was simple enough, a wish that she had suffered no ill effects from the episode, and signed "Jim." She refused to concede that part of her decision to keep the roses had been because of the signature. Subconsciously she knew that she was accepting the bouquet from Jim, the cattle thief, not from handsome James Corbett, the celebrity.

Nibbling at her lower lip, Brandy stepped back to survey the arrangement and nodded in satisfaction at the result. She had chosen the china vase that had been in her mother's family for generations. Its translucent cream finish with a delicate design of pink buds was a perfect foil for the darkly shimmering ruby red roses.

Carefully she picked up the vase and carried it into the living room. There she hesitated before deciding that the backdrop of the white wall behind the walnut stereo cabinet would better suit the bouquet than an open display on the coffee table in front the vibrantly green sofa.

She was just centering the vase on the stereo when the front door opened, and its closing was followed by the light footsteps of her mother.

"Hello, Brandy." The casual greeting was followed immediately by a delighted, "What beautiful roses! Where did you get them?"

"From Mr. Corbett," Brandy answered in a deliberately noncommittal voice.

"How thoughtful of him." Lenora Ames walked over to admire the full blooms.

"Hardly thoughtful, Mother," she shrugged, "I'm sure he was just trying to keep up his image."

"That's a very cynical remark coming from you." There was a thoughtful look in the green eyes that studied Brandy's composed mask.

"Not cynical really. The roses were only a polite

gesture. I'm sure Mr. Corbett just told his secretary or agent to send me some flowers. They're very pretty and I appreciate them, but I'm certainly not going to make a production out of receiving them," Brandy responded coolly.

"I wasn't suggesting that you should," Lenora said dryly.

Moving away from the vase of roses and the questioning eye of her mother, Brandy walked toward the kitchen. "I'll go start dinner. Where's Dad?"

"Putting the car in the garage. He'll be in shortly." There was a pause. "Brandy, what happened today?"

Halting in the kitchen archway, Brandy turned slightly. "Nothing happened. I went to work, that's all."

"Stewart and I were besieged with questions about the incident this weekend. You must have been, too. I know you feel some bitterness about the experience and I thought—"

"I do feel bitter," she agreed forcefully. "No one likes to be made fun of, and you know he must have found it terribly funny that I didn't know who he was. Everyone is making a big fuss of it, saying how romantic and thrilling it must have been. I found it humiliating." Pride tipped her chin to a more aggressive angle. "Now if you don't mind, I'll go fix dinner."

There was no protest from her mother or any further attempt to bring the conversation back to James Corbett. Her father, when he came in, commented that the roses were lovely, but never asked who had sent them. Brandy surmised that her mother had told him.

The next day, she deliberately omitted mentioning the bouquet to Karen. Her friend's imagination would have been immediately triggered by the gift of a dozen long-stemmed red roses. Karen would have undoubtedly read some significance in them, and Brandy was tired of her romantic flights of fantasy concerning James Corbett.

The furor caused by her escapade in the desert had finally trickled to an odd remark here and there by Thursday. The tension that stretched Brandy's nerves taut had eased. She no longer felt constantly on guard when a customer or acquaintance entered the shop. At last now she could finally believe that, in time, the whole episode would be forgotten.

By Thursday evening, with her parents busily preparing the content of their next day's classes in the large den, Brandy felt that life was beginning to return to normal. Sighing, she leaned back against the overstuffed cushions of the redwood chaise-lounge and tucked a hand behind her head.

The glare of the sun had abated as it lingered above the western hills and the enormous Papago Indian reservation that lay beyond them. A scarlet-pink hue was beginning to edge the yellow glow. The spectacular display of sunset colors had started.

From her vantage point on the southern side of the L-shaped patio that covered all of the south side of the house and part of the east, Brandy could view the magically silent yet colorfully explosive end of the day.

"With a view like this of sundown, why did you ride out into the desert?" a low voice inquired behind her.

Sitting upright with a start, she turned toward the voice. She hadn't heard the sliding glass doors open from the house to the patio. Yet there stood James Corbett.

This time there was no possibility she could mistake his identity. The only trace of the old Jim that she could see was in the glitter of his dark eyes and the latent impression of something dangerous. The beard was gone, revealing the carved cheek and jawline and the faint cleft in his chin while also exposing the cynically mocking grooves near his mouth. The faded denims were gone, too, and the sheepskin-lined suede vest and dust-covered shirt. No stained and dusty stetson covered the curling dark hair.

There was nothing disheveled and unkempt about him now. A silk shirt in understated colors of blue, cream yellow, and green molded his wide shoulders and chest, the long sleeves rolled up to reveal his tanned, muscled forearms. Snugly tailored slacks of pale blue covered his legs and thighs. The force of his magnetism was unmistakable, so compelling that Brandy marveled she had not guessed who he was before.

As the shock of seeing him again finally receded, she found her tongue. "H—how did you get here?" she asked weakly.

At her absence of greeting, his mouth shifted into a crooked line that wasn't exactly a smile. "Your mother let me in. She said you were out here watching the sunset ."

"Yes," she murmured as if he needed confirmation that she was on the patio. Disconcerted by the thudding of her heart at his unexpected appearance, she averted her gaze. "I received the flowers. Thank you." That sounded so abrupt and insincere that she wished she hadn't mentioned the roses.

"You're welcome." There was a faintly taunting inclination of his dark head. "May I sit down?"

"Yes, of course." Her hand gestured nervously for him to take his pick of the empty patio chairs.

To her dismay, he chose the one closest to the chaise-lounge where she was seated, the chair already angled to face her. As he sat down, she stood up and walked to one of the hardwood pillars that supported the beamed overhang shading most of the patio. The fingers of one hand closed over the rough wood. "This isn't a social visit, Mr. Corbett. Why have you come here?" She turned to look at him as she voiced the taut question, unaware that she was framed by the setting sun. Its golden flame ignited the amber curls of her hair.

"What makes you so positive that it isn't a social visit?" He tipped his head to one side, sooty lashes veiling the watchful look in his eyes.

Her mouth tightened as again she glanced away from his powerful features. "If you've come to see if

I weathered the ordeal satisfactorily last weekend, then the answer is yes, I have."

"I'm glad to hear that, Brandy," Jim replied diffidently.

The use of her given name grated across her already raw nerves. Mostly, she admitted silently, because when she wasn't looking at him and he spoke, she could almost believe it was Jim sitting there and not James Corbett. It was crazy to keep thinking of him as two different people.

Her fingers were pressed against the wood pillar and she stared at the contrast of golden tan flesh and the umber brown wood. "Now that I've reassured you on that point, Mr. Corbett, there isn't any need for you to prolong your visit out of politeness."

A low chuckle mocked her attempt to get rid of him. "I've never been accused of being a gentleman—I suspect it's because I'm not. So your thinly disguised invitation for me to leave isn't going to work."

Brandy pivoted sharply, an angry glare in her turquoise green eyes. "That I can believe, Mr. Corbett," she snapped. "I had proof of the fact that you aren't a gentleman, a fact I unfortunately forgot for a few minutes."

The hard, masculine mouth smiled lazily. "Finally we're getting to the point of my visit."

"Which is?" Brandy demanded harshly.

"I know you were hurt and upset when you discovered who I was last Sunday—"

"No one likes to be unwittingly made a fool," she broke in. "I know you found it vastly amusing that I didn't recognize you. The whole episode must have given you quite a few laughs these past few days. If an attack of conscience has brought you here to apologize, Mr. Corbett—"

"I haven't come to apologize," he interrupted coldly, "because I don't regret what I did. And if you call me Mr. Corbett one more time, you're going to have to face the consequences!"

Remembering his overpowering strength, Brandy realized that he was prepared to back up his threat. Although intimidated by the latent ruthless quality she knew he possessed, she refused to let him see.

"What would you like me to call you?" she asked with a defiant toss of her head.

His dark eyes narrowed thoughtfully. "You had no difficulty previously with calling me Jim."

"It was the only name I knew at the time, so I could call you little else," Brandy reminded him haughtily.

"And now there are a few other choice names you would like to use instead?" he taunted softly.

"I didn't say that," she retorted.

"No, you thought it." A dark brow arched arrogantly at the conclusion of his statement. "Haven't you wondered why I didn't tell you who I was?"

A brittle laugh broke from her lips. "I think I can guess."

"Can you?" His mouth twisted cynically as he surveyed her with cutting disdain. "Then I hope I don't bore you too much with my explanation. I know how palling it can be to hear what you already know."

Brandy had to look away from the shivering coldness of his gaze, to conceal her quivering chin. "By all means, explain," she insisted in a low voice to keep her voice from trembling. "I'm sure you'll make it interesting."

The air around her crackled with electricity. She knew she was goading him to anger, but she couldn't seem to stop herself. His deception had hurt deeply, and she had no intention of forgiving him easily.

"When you stumbled into camp that night," Jim spoke with iron control that Brandy couldn't help but admire in the face of her rudeness, "my first thought was that you were a fan and had followed me. There are women, mostly young girls, who get their kicks out of sleeping with celebrities, and they go to great lengths to achieve that goal. I had no way of knowing at the beginning whether you might be one of those."

That explained the anger that had blazed in his eyes when he saw her, Brandy realized, but she refused to be placated by the knowledge.

"You must have been disappointed when you discovered I wasn't," she commented. "It might have livened up the evening for you, one of the side benefits of being a celebrity."

"My profession," there was biting emphasis on the word, "is very rewarding in many ways, but not without payment. My personal life is more public knowledge than I would like. Which is why I tend to guard the privacy I do attain very jealously. I don't waste it on the so-called side benefits you referred to. If I want a woman's company, I choose who and when."

Verbally chastized, some of the starch went out of her rigid stand with its intent to keep her deaf to his explanation. "I understand," Brandy offered in a vaguely conciliatory tone.

"Then I hope you understand when I admit that I did find it amusing that you mistook me for a cattle rustler. It was so completely ridiculous that I knew it couldn't have been a trick to persuade me to let you stay the night." Wicked dancing lights gleamed in his eyes when Brandy gazed at him in astonishment, stunned that he would openly acknowledge that he found her lack of recognition amusing. "You were so absolutely convinced I was a rustler that I simply didn't know how to tell you the truth. And after a while, I didn't want to tell you."

"Oh, no, it was all too humorous," Brandy declared bitterly.

"Not humorous." With an effortless, animal grace, he pushed his long length out of the chair and walked to the wood pillar where Brandy stood. Her head tipped back to gaze into his face, so compelling in its rugged, chiseled lines and sheer maleness. "It wasn't because I found your ignorance laughable, Brandy. For the first time in a very long while, I was another human being. It was a pleasant change."

Breathing in shakily, she leaned back against the pillar. His explanation was undoing all the imagined insults and humiliation she thought she had suffered.

"I would have found out eventually who you were."

"Yes, I think I knew at the back of my mind that you would," he admitted, his velvet dark gaze not leaving her face. "But in the beginning, I planned to merely leave you close to your home where the search party could easily find you. The sandstorm changed that."

"Why?" Brandy asked, remembering that he had resisted her attempt to help him escape when they had first seen the helicopter.

"Because I recognized the helicopter as belonging to Saguarro Ranch. I knew it could have been enlisted in search for you, but I doubted that Don Peters, who is for all practical purposes my manager, would have volunteered his services. The fact that he was in the helicopter meant they were looking for me as well. The man has enough problems with his ulcers without me giving him more just to satisfy a foolish whim."

He was standing in front of her, tall and strong and vitally attractive. A foot and more separated them, yet the sensation remained that he was disturbingly close. Brandy felt herself surrendering and tore her gaze away from his face.

"It wasn't fair of you not to tell me who you were," she protested, but with none of her former belligerence.

"When I saw the helicopter, I realized I would have no choice." A hand moved to the pillar beside her golden curls soft and feathery about her face. "There wasn't time before it landed to tell you and explain why I hadn't told you before. I hoped I would be able to speak to you privately after we arrived at your home, but shortly after we got on board the helicopter you recognized me, didn't you?"

His arm, tanned a teak brown and sinewy strong, was only inches from the soft flesh of her golden cheek. Wispy strands of her honey-colored hair were tangled in the curling dark hairs on his arm. Her tip-tilted nose was pointed downward, as she found she was unable to meet the disconcerting directness of his gaze.

"Yes, I did," she admitted. "I heard the man ... your manager ... refer to you as Corbett. That's when I realized who you were."

Peering at him through the tawny veil of her lashes, she saw a distantness close over his expression, hardening it slightly while making him look withdrawn and aloof.

"If you'd seen the look that came into your eyes when you recognized me," one corner of his mouth lifted in a humorless smile, "you would understand why I put off telling you."

"What do you mean?" she raised her head, confused by his comment.

"In your eyes, I suddenly wasn't human any more. It was some celluloid image you were seeing," he stated. "And for a while, I didn't care what reason you thought I had for not telling you the truth."

She wanted very much to believe what he was saying—she was only now beginning to discover how much. Searching the obisidian darkness of his eyes, she tried to find a flaw. "And now you do?" she asked for confirmation in a wary voice.

"You still can't trust me, can you?" His dark head tipped to the side, studying her hesitant expression with a resigned gentleness.

"I haven't had much cause," she defended.

"I wouldn't say that," he denied with a faint smile. "I think my behavior was quite exemplary during the time we spent together."

"Well ... yes, it was," she admitted.

"Then have dinner with me on Saturday night." The grooves around his mouth deepened.

"I ... I beg your pardon?" Brandy was certain Jim didn't mean what he had just said.

"I said, have dinner with me Saturday night."

"But why?"

"Why do you think?" he countered with maddening ease. "Because I want to have dinner with you, of course."

Her forehead smoothed as she nervously moistened her lips. "You mustn't feel obliged to take me to dinner. I quite understand everything now and there isn't any need for you to make this gesture."

"Brandy, I'm not a gentleman. I don't make gestures," he answered in a patiently indulgent tone.

That enigmatic light in his dark eyes was making her believe things that he didn't mean. Brandy looked hurriedly away, the vein in her neck beating a rapid tattoo. His charismatic charm was going to her head. In another minute, he was going to succeed in talking her into accepting his invitation. Her inclination was to accept. Then darting him a sideways glance, she suddenly realized how foolish she was being. He was James Corbett. Their two worlds barely touched.

Suddenly the soft flesh of her upper arm was seized in a punishing grip. The patiently amused line of his mouth had hardened into anger as he jerked her on to tiptoe inches from his chest. The harsh glitter of his eyes raked her face.

"Stop looking at me that way!" he growled.

Faltering under his censorious gaze, Brandy shook her head weakly. "I can't help it."

"Dammit, Brandy!" The pressure of his fingers eased, letting her stand before him, although he didn't release her. He sighed with exasperation.

"What do I have to do to make you understand?"

"I can't forget who you are," she protested. "And I'm flattered that you should want to have dinner with me, but—"

"Flattered!" The word curled savagely sarcastic from his hard mouth. "I'm not some god or king bestowing a favor on you."

"Then what do you want me to say?" Brandy cried in a kind of despairing anger. "If you want a simple yes or no, then the answer is no! Now please let me go!"

His hands fell swiftly away as if her flesh revolted

him. Before he could change his mind, she moved away from the pillar to put a safer distance between them. She kept her back toward him to hide her quivering chin and the tears that scalded her eyes.

Everything was so crazy. She wanted to turn around and take back her answer, even though every ounce of logic insisted she had made the right decision. An inner voice argued for her to accept. It was only a dinner invitation; she could go, just for the experience of dating a celebrity. It would be something to tell her children some day. But she couldn't treat it as a lark. Some instinct warned her that no time spent with Jim Corbett could ever be treated so casually.

"The next time, Brandy," his voice when he spoke was controlled and calm, "things will be different."

Brandy glanced over her shoulder, the inner torment partially mirrored in her shimmering turquoise eyes. "No, Mr. Corbett, they won't," she said firmly.

Holding her gaze for a long moment, he said nothing, then he pivoted on his heel and exited through the sliding glass doors. She didn't feel any relief when he had gone. Jim Corbett did not make idle statements, and she knew she hadn't seen the last of him.

ALL WEEKEND Brandy was jumping at the sound of every car driving by the house. Each ring of the telephone made her heart stop beating, but by Monday morning Jim had still made no effort to contact her. As each day of the week dragged by, she could not help wondering if perhaps he had decided she wasn't worth wasting his time over. She realized she was much more feminine than she had thought. Even though she didn't want to go out with him, she wanted him to keep asking.

Although more than a week had gone by without her hearing from him, that didn't mean she hadn't heard about Jim Corbett. Karen, blithely unaware of his visit and his invitation to dinner, had avidly passed on every tidbit of gossip she had either read in the paper or heard from unknown sources.

So it was from her girl friend that Brandy learned of the torrid affair that had sprung up between Jim Corbett and LaRaine Evans, one of the supporting actresses in the movie being filmed at Old Tucson. One newspaper clipping Karen had included a photograph of the two together, the vivacious brunette nestled under the crook of Jim's arm. A stab of pure envy had pierced Brandy's heart at the sight of it.

The jabbing sensation didn't lessen when she learned, from Karen of course, that the couple had spent the previous weekend in the border town of Nogales, an hour's drive south of Tucson. When she was told that along with seeing the sights in Mexico they had attended a bullfight, she cattily decided that the brunette looked like the bloodthirsty type that would enjoy such a spectacle.

With the passage of the second weekend and no word, Brandy acknowledge that she had seen the last of Jim Corbett. What had she expected, she asked herself as she carried the lightweight step-ladder from the back room of the shop. Attractive in a wholesome way she might be, but she couldn't compete with the stunningly sensuous and vibrantly alive LaRaine Evans.

"What are you going to do with that ladder, Brandy?" Karen frowned and jumped forward to move a large ceramic statue of a cherub out of Brandy's way.

"I decided it was time to rearrange the macramé display." She maneuvered the cumbersome length of the ladder safely by the statue. Her path to the hanging pottery suspended by creatively knotted and colorful rope strands was now clear of obstacles. "We've had the same things up since April, and people like to see something new."

"Want some help?"

"I think I can manage," Brandy replied, concentrating on setting up the ladder without knocking any of the pots.

"I'll take care of the customers and when Mrs. Phillips comes back from lunch, I'll give you a hand so you don't have to keep running up and down the ladder. If she comes back from lunch, that is," Karen added with a speaking roll of her eyes. "If she didn't have faithful, hardworking employees like us, I don't know how she'd make a living out of this store. She's never here half the time."

"That's precisely why she hired us, so she wouldn't have to be," Brandy laughed as she climbed the ladder, dodging the pots that swung about her head.

"Oh, oh," Karen murmured, "Mrs. Goodwin has just walked in. She ordered a special shade of yarn for an afghan she's making. It wasn't in the last shipment and Mrs. Phillips promised her faithfully we would have it by today."

"Good luck," Brandy whispered as her friend moved reluctantly toward the woman.

Sitting precariously on the top step, nearly hidden from view by the fibrous curtain of macramé hangings, Brandy began selecting which ones would be replaced or their appearance altered by the insertion of a differently colored or patterned ceramic pot.

Someone else entered the shop, but since she knew Karen would be free in a few minutes to wait on the new customer, she didn't let her attention stray from her task. Her hand froze on the ceiling hook of a hanging she had been about to remove when she heard the man's voice.

"I'd like to look at some of your leather tooling equipment." The deep, husky voice belonged to none other than Jim Corbett.

"O—Of course, Mr. Corbett," Karen stammered her disbelief at the identity of her customer.

Carefully peering through the colored and beaded hangings so as not to draw attention to herself, Brandy saw him as he removed the sunglasses and turned to follow Karen. She held her breath. Had he discovered she worked here and come to see her? It couldn't be possible, but she knew that she was desperately hoping it was.

Karen was all thumbs when they reached the leather counter, nearly dropping the tray of tools he asked to see on the floor. Then when he helped her, she nearly swooned—and Brandy didn't blame her. Jim looked much handsomer than she remembered, if that was possible, and so casual and at ease.

Not daring to move, afraid that if he hadn't come to see her, it might prove embarrassing, she waited for him to mention her name. The string curtain of macramé concealed her from view.

"Do...do you work in leather, Mr. Corbett?" Karen asked.

He glanced up from the tool he was inspecting and smiled faintly. "It's a hobby of mine. I like working with my hands."

"I imagine it's a good way to relax after filming all day," her friend suggested agreeably. As some of the shock receded at coming face to face with James Corbett, Karen's more garrulous personality began asserting itself. "You don't know what a thrill it is for me to meet you, Mr. Corbett. I've been a fan of yours for a long time. I've seen all of your movies, some of them more than once."

"Thank you. I hope you enjoyed them," his dark head nodded in near indifference.

"Oh, I did!" Karen assured him with a rush. "I can hardly wait until the one you're filming here is released, so I can go see it. It must be a very exciting business."

"In some ways," he agreed, but Brandy detected a

note of dry cynicism. "In others, it's much more tedious than your job."

"I find that hard to believe," Karen laughed, self-consciously flicking her flame-colored hair behind her shoulder. "But then I've never seen a movie being made before."

Selecting the tools he wanted from the array Karen had shown him, Jim handed them to her so she could ring up his purchase. Brandy decided his presence in the store had nothing to do with her and could only hope now that Karen wouldn't mention her name. Perhaps her friend would still be too flustered to remember her.

"Would you like a behind the scenes look at a movie being filmed, Miss—?" he inquired as he paid for the tools.

"It's Justin, Karen Justin," she introduced herself quickly. "Would I ever like that!"

"I could arrange for you to have a pass one day next week if you're free?" he offered indulgently.

"Oh, yes. The shop is closed Thursday afternoons," Karen declared excitedly.

"Then perhaps if you can persuade Miss Ames to come down off her perch, she might like to join you." With that Jim turned, his mocking gaze looking directly at the curtain of filaments behind which Brandy was hiding.

The unexpected use of her name startled her so much that she jerked convulsively backward, bumping against the hangings and sending them banging into each other. She had to grab hold of the ladder to keep from falling. Luckily she was spared that embarrassment as she regained her balance and awkwardly descended the ladder. Jim was waiting at the bottom, his dark eyes laughing at the red stain in her cheeks.

"Did you really think you were hidden up there?" he murmured.

"I wasn't trying to hide," Brandy denied self-consciously, "I was doing some rearranging of the display."

Glancing warily at Karen, she caught the knowing glitter in her friend's eyes, and was left in little doubt as to what she was thinking.

"I see, you were just working quietly," he smiled crookedly. "Since you were so busily occupied, maybe I should repeat the invitation I extended to Miss Justin."

Brandy couldn't admit to eavesdropping. "What invitation was that, Mr. Corbett?"

Her formal reference to him brought a slight narrowing of his gaze, a silent reprimand to remind her of his previous warning.

"I offered to obtain a pass for you and Miss Justin so that you'd be permitted on the set while the movie is being filmed. Your friend mentioned that the shop would be closed next Thursday afternoon—I'll arrange it for then if that's satisfactory." The challenge in his expression was undeniable.

Brandy remembered his parting statement when he visited her home that the next time things would be different. She wanted to refuse the invitation out of sheer perversity, while at the same time she wanted to accept with equal intensity. The conflict must have been written in her face.

"Of course it's satisfactory," Karen spoke up, her eyes pleading with Brandy not to throw away this once-in-a-lifetime opportunity.

"Yes," Brandy agreed with a small, reluctant sigh, "Thursday will be fine."

"Good." There was a suggestion of arrogant triumph in the faint smile that curved the masculine mouth. "I'll make all the necessary arrangements. Just check in at the gate when you arrive and everything will be taken care of for you."

"Thank you very much, Mr. Corbett," Karen smiled broadly. "This is really kind of you."

"It's my pleasure." But the darting look at Brandy reaffirmed what she already knew. Kindness had nothing to do with it. He was proving his point that he always got what he wanted.

As he wished them goodbye, Brandy realized how very experienced he was at handling women. First he had kept her in suspense for nearly two weeks without contacting her at all. Then, just about the time when she decided she wouldn't see him again and was regretting she hadn't taken advantage of his invitation, he had appeared.

There had been no grounds to refuse the invitation he offered the second time; Jim had seen to that. He did not suggest a possibly intimate evening. On the contrary, he had invited her girl friend to come along in case Brandy felt the necessity of a chaperone. And secondly, it was a daytime invitation for a tour of the movie set in Old Tucson. Brandy had no doubts that it would be an interesting and informative outing and, by its very nature, innocent.

He had changed the set of circumstances and she had accepted without a protest. Well, it was what she had been secretly wanting, regardless of how illogical it was. Karen was probably right. It was a chance in a lifetime and she might as well enjoy it.

If only Thursday afternoon didn't seem so far off, she thought silently. There was too much time to think.

CHAPTER FIVE

"I'M SO EXCITED! Look at the way I'm shaking," Karen held out a trembling hand to confirm her statement.

"Relax," Brandy smiled, but the palms of her hands were clammy with nervous perspiration and an army of butterflies was fluttering in her stomach.

Karen's car was parked in the parking lot with other tourists' vehicles and they were walking to the entrance building that would admit them to Old Tucson, a recreated town of the Old West days.

"I hope I don't talk too much," Karen sighed, then worriedly, "I hope he hasn't forgotten we're coming today."

"He hasn't," Brandy assured her promptly.

"Of course not." There was a wry shake of her Titian head. "Not with you along, he won't forget. Especially when you consider the trouble he went to to get you here. Every time I think about you turning down a date with James Corbett, I become more convinced that you must have had rocks in your head."

After he had left the shop on Monday, Brandy had told Karen about his visit to her home, hoping to minimize the second invitation. She had been severely scolded for keeping it a secret all this time, and her sanity doubted.

"We've been all through this before," Brandy protested in self-defense. "Besides, what could I possibly have in common with a movie star?"

"Who cares, for heaven's sake!" The chiding exclamation was accompanied by an exasperated sigh. "And if you never go out with him, you're never going to know whether you do or not. I only hope you haven't lost him to that Evans girl."

"I haven't had him, so I couldn't have lost him," Brandy pointed out, but there was a twinge of pain in her midriff.

Karen ignored the accuracy of that observation. "Maybe they quarreled and he's turning to you for consolation. It might explain why he waited so long before seeing you again."

"It's possible." All too clearly possible, although the idea that a man as confident and self-possessed as Jim might need consoling did sound unusual.

As they stepped out of the brilliance of the mid-day sun into the comparative darkness of the small entry building, they had to pause inside the threshold until their eyes adjusted to the dimmer light. An older couple was at the ticket window, so they moved to take their place in line behind them.

A balding man in an old-fashioned starched white shirt with a garter around one sleeve and red braces down the front smiled blandly as they approached the ticket window.

"Good afternoon, ladies," he greeted them with professional cheerfulness.

Brandy's throat became parched, a sudden attack of nerves making her incapable of speech, but Karen suffered no such difficulty.

"I believe Mr. Corbett left some passes for us?" she began. "I'm ...."

The politeness in his expression was immediately replaced by a friendly warmth. "You'd be Miss Justin and Miss Ames," he identified them before Karen had a chance. The gleam in his light blue eyes lingered on Brandy for a speculative moment. "He told me you would be coming. If you'll wait a few minutes, I'll get somebody to take you through."

"Thanks, we appreciate that," Karen smiled as they jointly started to move to one side so that they wouldn't hold up the other people waiting in line.

"Miss Ames," the man's voice halted Brandy, "the picture in the paper didn't do you justice. You're much prettier."

There was only one photograph he could be referring to, the one taken after she and Jim had been rescued in the desert. Brandy had thought that incident would have been forgotten after all this time, or at least that no one would remember her by name. There was an uncomfortable surge of warmth in her neck at what the man might be thinking at this moment, with the special passes being arranged for them by Jim.

"Thank you," she responded to his compliment self-consciously, and moved hurriedly away from the window.

While they waited, she and Karen studied the small billboards with photographs of the more well known movies and television series that had been filmed in Old Tucson. Only a few minutes passed before the ticket clerk was signaling them to come forward.

On the other side of the turnstile a man waited, dressed in cowboy gear with a star pinned to his chest and a gun strapped around his hips. The illusion of an Old West town marshal was negated by the dark sunglasses he wore and the walkie-talkie he carried in his left hand. The balding man stepped out of the ticket booth to introduce the girls to their picturesque escort.

"This is Dick Murphy. He'll take you through to the movie set. Dick," he turned to the man, a bright twinkle in his eyes, "this is Miss Ames and Miss Justin. They're guests of Mr. Corbett, so you take real good care of them."

"Ladies." The man called Dick Murphy touched the front brim of his hat in acknowledgment, then motioned them through the turnstile. "Follow me, please."

"We're really getting the VIP treatment, aren't we?" Karen whispered in a faintly giggling voice.

Brandy gave her a silencing look and didn't reply as they started up the path of hard-packed sand to the main street of town. A tall fence hid the parking lot from view, letting them walk back into time with the ageless Tucson Mountains in the distance to form a backdrop for the scene.

"Since you girls are from Tucson," Dick Murphy spoke, "I imagine you know most of the town was built back in 1939 for the film *Arizona*. Then it was abandoned for quite a few years."

"I had heard that," Karen answered. "Actually Brandy ... Miss Ames is from Tucson. I've only been here for a couple of years. I'm originally from Breckenridge, Colorado."

"That's in the middle of the Rockies, quite a change of scenery and climate," the man observed with a pleasant smile.

"You're telling me!" Karen grimaced. Then she glanced around at the tourists wandering along the broad sidewalks. "I've never been out here when they've been filming a movie. How do they keep all the people out of the way?"

"They close the area from the public when they're shooting a particular scene," he explained.

Brandy looked curiously ahead of her. "Where are they filming today?"

"In the little Mexican village area." His head bobbed in an easterly direction to indicate its location.

At the next narrow road leading in that direction, Dick Murphy turned, walking around the barricade that blocked the road. A security guard was standing on the other side, dressed in similar attire to that Dick wore. The man nodded briefly to the trio as they passed.

Leaving the main street, the buildings changed from wooden western fronts, painted to look antique and weathered, to the dull tan of adobe brick. Ahead, Brandy could see and hear activity going on. Then, as they drew nearer, the motion and voices stopped, and neither she nor Karen needed to be told that filming had begun.

Quietly they approached the statuelike group gazing intently at the action going on in front of the cameras. The technicians and onlookers blocked their view of the actors. Cranes held cameras and cameramen aloft, while below more equipment was joined in a complex network of wires.

Brandy was only absently aware of what was going on. Her concentration was focused on locating Jim Corbett. He might be one of the actors in the scene, but it was also possible that he was watching from the sidelines.

At the far end she saw him. His shoulder leaned against a brick building, the powerfully defined chin and jaw cupped thoughtfully in his left hand as he watched the scene unfolding. A thumb was hooked in the waistband of his blue levis, one leg slightly bent at the knee in a relaxed pose.

Yet even with the brim of his brown hat pulled low on his forehead to shade his eyes from the glare of the sun, Brandy could sense the piercing watchfulness of his dark eyes. When he was dressed in Western gear that brought to mind the lawless time of the frontier, the ruthless, dangerous quality about him was heightened.

Although minus the beard, Jim looked very much

like the man she had met in the desert, intimidatingly male and strongly independent. There was gentleness in him, though he had insisted he was no gentleman.

Her heart skipped a beat as she saw him straighten and turn in her direction. A smile of greeting curved her lips in anticipation of the moment when he would see her, but his gaze didn't encounter hers.

He started walking in her general direction, the object of his attention between them. Other people milled about, signaling an end of that film take. He stopped behind a man in dark-rimmed glasses with a pen tucked behind one ear, and wearing a white shirt that had seen fresher days.

Almost instantly the two men were joined by a raven-haired woman, the object of Jim's attention. Brandy could understand why when she saw the low-cut peasant blouse and the creamy-gold shoulders it revealed. A full skirt swung about her ankles, a brilliant shade of red material that complimented her dark looks and artfully molded the sensuous curve of her hips.

With a sinking heart Brandy recognized the vivaciously beautiful woman as LaRaine Evans, whose name had been romantically coupled with Jim's in the past two weeks. Her arm slipped quite familiarly around his waist, and she bestowed on him a dazzling smile before turning her attention to the second man. By this time Brandy had decided that he was the director of the film, judging by the quiet yet brisk way his orders were being given.

An animated discussion ensued; at least animated on the woman's part, Brandy qualified. She doubted if the actress was ever anything else but animated. The woman was a black flame, a blaze that could never appear subdued.

What a pair they made standing together like that, she thought with an envious sigh. Their dark looks complemented each other, each compellingly attractive. No wonder their names were linked—they made a perfect couple.

Beside her, she was aware of Dick Murphy explaining to Karen what was happening on the set now, but the activity of the film crew didn't interest Brandy. Her whole attention was centered on Jim as she became conscious of a forlorn ache in her heart.

How foolish she had been to think she might have attracted Jim! She was about to look away in despair when her gaze was met by his. Unconsciously she held her breath, wondering if it was actually her that he was looking at or someone else perhaps standing behind her. There was a barely perceptible nod of his head in acknowledgment before he glanced at the upturned face of the brunette.

Brandy turned quickly away, not wanting him to realize how much she had wanted Jim to notice her. The irregularity of her breathing was matched by the erratic rhythm of her heart. Yet even with her head averted, her gaze kept sliding back to him.

Her heart leaped crazily when she saw Jim separate himself from the brunette. She tried frantically to concentrate on what Dick Murphy was telling Karen, but she was only conscious of the tall figure making his way toward them. Although she pretended surprise, she knew the exact instant he reached them.

"I see you made it safely here." His dark eyes mocked her less than genuine expression.

"Yes, we did." Brandy smiled nervously. "Thank you for inviting us. Karen and I are really finding it all fascinating." She immediately included her friend in case Jim might think that she had ever imagined the invitation had been issued more for herself than for her and Karen together.

"Oh, yes," Karen agreed enthusiastically. "Dick—Mr. Murphy has been explaining everything to us. I always knew movie-making was complex and technical, but the fine detail of it all escaped me."

"I hope you find the rest of your tour equally informative," Jim stated dryly as he noted the faint pink in Brandy's cheeks. Then his attention shifted to their escort. "Thanks for looking after them for me, Dick."

"Any time, Jim," the man replied, touching his hat brim as he wished each of the girls goodbye.

Brandy cast an apprehensive glance at Jim, realizing that he would act as their guide. When he had issued the invitation at the shop, she had thought that might be the case. Later she had dismissed it, arguing that he would probably be working himself. The knowing glint in his eyes said he knew exactly what was going on in her mind.

"He's good-looking, isn't he?" Karen observed with a resigned sigh. Brandy glanced at her girl friend in alarm, then realized she was referring to Dick Murphy and not the disturbing man standing beside her. "Too bad he's wearing a wedding ring," she added, staring after the departing figure with a wistful expression on her face. She looked at Brandy, a wry grimace pulling up one corner of her mouth. "But then that's just my luck, isn't it?"

"I think you could put Dick on the eligible list," Jim told her in a dryly amused tone. "He lost his wife a year ago in a car accident."

"That's too bad." Karen murmured with genuine sincerity, but a gleam of hope appeared in her brown eyes.

"Aren't you working today?" Brandy fought to maintain her composure that was fast disintegrating under his mocking regard.

"Not today." The lines around his mouth deepened. "I thought I would volunteer my expert services to show you around."

"That's kind of you," Brandy said self-consciously.

"Isn't it?" he mocked.

"Darling!" A female voice interrupted them, all husky and warm, vibrating with a sensual undertone. LaRaine Evans was curling her arm possessively through Jim's, totally ignoring Brandy and Karen as she claimed his attention. "How about joining me in something tall and cold and wet?"

Up close, the actress was even more stunningly

beautiful than she had appeared at a distance. Dancing eyes of dark velvet offered an entirely different invitation as she gazed at Jim. He didn't attempt to deny her claim of ownership.

"Sorry." A mockingly indulgent smile edged his mouth. "Not this time. I have guests." He looked pointedly to Brandy and Karen.

"Guests?" LaRaine Evans echoed, rounded brown eyes swinging to them with open curiosity. The request for an introduction couldn't have been more obvious if she had stated it.

A cynically humorous light entered Jim's eyes as he obliged. "LaRaine, this is Karen Justin and Brandy Ames," he introduced. "This talented and beautiful actress is one of my co-stars, LaRaine Evans."

"And a friend, darling," the brunette laughed throatily to coyly insinuate a closer relationship between them.

Brandy's stomach churned into a ball of painful knots at the intimate look the actress gave him. The woman was as subtle as a steamroller.

"Whatever." Jim shrugged, refusing to attach a label to their relationship. There was a faint tightening of the brunette's mouth, as if his noncommittal reply displeased her. It lasted for a fleeting second and was gone.

"Brandy—that's a very unusual name." Artificially long lashes swept up as LaRaine Evans turned her attention to Brandy.

"Yes, it is unusual," Brandy agreed without

110

offering any explanation for her parents' choice. There was little, except that her mother had liked it.

"Of course!" A smile flashed across the brunette's face. "I know why it's so familiar now. You must be the girl who spent the night on the desert with Jim."

The way she said "girl" made Brandy feel that she had worn her first pair of nylons last week. Temper flared briefly in her turquoise green eyes before she veiled it and glanced at Jim.

"Yes, that's right," she admitted, a hint of suggestive warmth in her voice. She deliberately didn't add any more, guessing that the actress's imagination was vivid enough to paint whatever picture she wanted.

An arrogant brow arched coldly at Brandy before LaRaine tipped her raven head back to gaze at Jim. "You didn't tell me she was such a pretty little thing," she accused, her lower lip jutting out in a very alluring pout.

"No, I didn't," he agreed smoothly. "But I'm hardly likely to broadcast that Brandy was such a captivating and lovely companion."

LaRaine's expression stiffened at the caressing quality in his low voice, but she smiled quickly to conceal her displeasure. "Careful, Jim, or you'll put all sorts of silly ideas in her head."

"Will I?" His dark eyes glinted wickedly at Brandy's flushed cheeks. "I hope so," he added calmly.

"You're impossible!" LaRaine declared, tempestuous fires blazing in her eyes.

"You're learning," he drawled, glancing with open challenge at her ill-concealed expression of irritation. "You'd better go and get your cold drink while Bill is still inclined to let you have a break."

Red lips were pressed tightly together. "I think I'll do that," she said coldly, releasing his arm and whirling away with a haughty toss of her blue-black hair.

"Whew—for a minute, I thought she was going to explode," Karen whispered to Brandy. "Talk about fireworks!"

Her comment hadn't been meant for Jim to hear, but he did. "The next segment of the scene they're shooting calls for LaRaine's character to lose her temper. She should do it quite naturally, don't you think?" Jim suggested, an audacious twinkle in his eyes.

Brandy couldn't help letting a faint smile of agreement tug at the corners of her mouth, while Karen suggested, "It won't be a case of acting as much as it will be reacting."

Jim didn't appear upset that LaRaine was angry, and Brandy wondered if it had been his intention from the beginning to use her to make the actress jealous. If they had quarreled as Karen had suggested earlier, perhaps it was because the brunette had been taking him too much for granted. He wasn't the type to be dominated by anyone, male or female.

"Since they're still blocking camera angles for the next scene," Jim said, "I'll take you over to the sound stage and show you some of the props and tricks of the trade."

112

Stepping between them, he guided them back toward the main street, a hand resting with light but firm pressure on the back of Brandy's waist. As they passed the barricade, tourists who were aware that a movie was being filmed in the off-limits section of the western town looked curiously at them to see if they could recognize the privileged trio which had so easily been allowed entrance.

Recognition of James Corbett whispered through them like a breeze rippling through prairie grass. Those who had cameras immediately snapped pictures, regardless of the distance or angle, to prove to the folks back home that they had really seen a movie star.

Jim appeared oblivious to the stir he was causing, his purposeful stride neither rushing nor slowing as he escorted Karen and Brandy past the ice cream parlor. Brandy guessed that he was probably accustomed to it. Although nothing in his attitude invited closer contact, one young girl rushed toward them, anxiously thrusting a pen and paper toward him.

"Could I have your autograph, please, Mr. Corbett?" she breathed, gazing at him through dazed, unbelieving eyes.

Taking the paper and pen, he smiled at the young girl pleasantly, though still with a suggestion of aloofness. Bold, sure strokes spelled his name on the paper, completely legible with no pretentious flourishes.

"Thank you," the girl gushed when he had handed the

113

paper back, holding it almost reverently in her hand.

"That's quite all right." Briefly he touched his hat. "Excuse me."

His hand was again on the back of Brandy's waist, bringing her level with him after she had drifted a half step behind him. She rather liked the sensation of pride that his action aroused inside her, as though he wanted the onlookers to know she was with him. Karen must have noticed the action, too, because she caught Brandy's eye and winked knowingly. Self-conscious, Brandy averted her gaze.

An employee of Old Tucson unlocked the door to the soundstage, which was housed in a building whose exterior matched the Old West design of the rest of the town. Inside, high ceilings stretched spaciously above their heads, and lighting equipment hung from the rafters.

There was no dividing wall in the large barnlike room, but it was sectioned by different sets. The one they proceeded to was an old-fashioned saloon with the long wooden bar stretching the length of one wall. Behind the bar was a large mirror flanked by shelves containing liquor bottles and glasses. Above the mirror hung a large painting of a fulsomely curved woman scantily covered by a pink robe reclining on a divan.

A second side of the room had swinging doors and large-paned windows. They gave the illusion that the main street of town was directly outside. Actually it was a realistic painting of the town's street. The third

114

wall of the U-shaped room had a series of doors that seemed to lead to back rooms and a staircase leading to the second-floor hall with more doors supposedly leading to second-floor rooms. From Brandy's position she could see there was nothing beyond the doors except steps leading down from the second floor on the outside of the set.

The center of the room was cluttered with tables and chairs. All of them looked battered and worn. A deck of cards sat on one table with neat stacks of poker chips, and a roulette wheel was toward the back of the room.

"The sets you see in here," Jim explained, "are where we shoot the interior scenes. This saloon, for example, has been used countless times for different movies. The public generally doesn't recognize it because the decor is changed or we rearrange the door on another wall or have the stairs leading to the second floor in a different place. It makes it very easy to duplicate the set in Hollywood, if another take is needed after we've left the location."

"It's so small, though," Karen commented.

"A camera makes everything look larger. That and the fact that the camera only shows you one section of the room at a time creates the illusion that the room is large. It's convenient because several small sets can be reconstructed and the viewer is rarely aware of how small they are." He paused, a dancing gleam in his dark eyes. "The only drawback to the camera making things larger is for the actresses. The camera gives them ten extra pounds whether they want them or not. It's the main reason they constantly diet."

"I don't blame them," Karen laughed shortly. "Nobody needs ten extra pounds unless they're Twiggy."

"As for the props, I imagine you know all about the breakaway furniture that gets broken over people's heads. And the breakaway bottles," he added. "They used to be made of candy, but too many of the technicians and acting crew were eating the props, so they use another substance now. Iced tea is used in place of hard liquor for drinks, except for beer—no one has come up with a substitute that looks enough like it and can keep a head of foam. As long as the beer is warm, the foam stays. If you've ever tasted warm beer, you know why the beer is only occasionally sipped by the actor." Jim smiled. "Unless, of course, the actor is English."

With his hand he gestured for them to move to the far end of the building.

"That's the interior of the sheriff's office." Jim identified the stage set they were passing. "This next one," their destination, "is used for scenes shot in the interior of a house. Right now, it's a dining room, but by changing the furniture and curtains it can be transformed into any room."

This three-walled interior set was unique in that it continued into an outside desert scene. The floor of the building was covered with realistic-looking sand and shrubs, and a large saguarro cactus stood guard

116

near the outside wall of the room. A scenic backdrop had been painted to continue the desert landscape.

"Isn't there enough desert outdoors to satisfy you?" Brandy frowned curiously.

"More than enough, but occasionally the script calls for a night sequence. Thank heaven, we don't film at night. The cameraman puts a special filter over his lens and the scene becomes night," he explained. "Or it might be a sunrise or sunset that's needed, then the special effects men use a combination of lighting to duplicate it. That way the sunset will last as long as it takes for the actors to do the scene right."

"I was certain you were ging to say it was used in rainy weather," Karen laughed.

"The heat and blowing sand are about the only complaints that can be made about Arizona weather. The heat you suffer through. The blowing sand does bring us indoors, but rain is rarely the cause. Usually it has to be manufactured out here."

"What do you use for rain? A garden hose and a fan?" Brandy asked, finding it all very fascinating.

"Well," one corner of his mouth tilted upwards, "I suppose that sounds logical except for one problem. Falling water doesn't photograph very well on a camera. When you see it raining in a movie, it's generally raining milk. On film, it looks like water."

"You're kidding!" Karen stared at him sceptically.

"I'm not," Jim promised with a deepening smile. "I'm afraid Gene Kelly danced and sang in the milk, not the rain."

117

"You're destroying all my illusions," Karen moaned in mock despair.

Jim laughed, a rich, deep sound that sent shivers of pleasure down Brandy's spine. She joined in, a captive of the charming side of this compellingly handsome man.

"Then I'll take you on to the wardrobe department, where you'll see some true artists at work," he offered.

CHAPTER SIX

AT THE WARDROBE department, an older woman gladly showed Karen and Brandy some of the clothes that would be worn in the film, at Jim's request. The sketches had all been completed weeks ago, faithful reproductions of the dress for men and women in that particular era and part of the country. The costumes were all individually sewn and fitted to the person who would be wearing them.

The wardrobe personnel on location were mainly to keep track of the costumes and be certain they were ready when they were needed. A seamstress took care of any last-minute alterations or repaired any rips or tears that occurred during filming.

From Wardrobe, Jim took them to the stables where the animals used in the film were kept; mostly they were horses, with an occasional burro or mule. A nearby rancher supplied a herd of cattle when they were needed. All of the mounts were trained stock, accustomed to crowds and the bustle of the camera crew.

One pathetic-looking horse in the corral caught Brandy's eye. He looked so out of place with the other sleek and trim stock that she had seen. There was no healthy gloss to his coat and a faint outline of his ribs could be seen.

"Jim, what's the matter with that horse?" Brandy used his first name quite unconsciously. Not even when his gaze focused with warm thoughtfulness on her face did she realize what she had done to evoke such a disturbing appraisal.

"Nothing is the matter with him any more. He was never sick, just underfed," he replied.

"You'll have the Humane Society breathing down your necks if they saw him," she commented.

"That's where he was found." His mouth curved crookedly at her curious glance. "It took a lot of searching before we could find such a poor excuse of a horse."

"Why did you need him?"

"In the film, the character I portray has a grueling ride through the desert. At the end of the ride, my horse was supposed to be on its last legs. I wasn't supposed to look too much better. That's the reason for the beard I'd grown when you met me. Luckily they got those scenes out of the way first." He rubbed his smoothly shaven jaw as if the memory of the disheveled beard made him itch. "You're looking at the horse, or a healthier version of the same."

"What's going to happen to him now?" Brandy leaned against the corral fence, staring compassionately at the horse.

"He's become something of a pet. Harry, the stock contractor, seems to think he has a chance to make it in the movies when his looks improve. The horse gobbles up any attention he receives almost as he eats

120

his corn and oats," Jim told her. "If he doesn't, I imagine Harry will probably sell him to someone who'll take care of him."

"I hope so," she declared.

"Let's go over in the shade and have a cold drink," he suggested.

The cool shadow cast by the barnlike stable was already being used as a sun shelter by some of the film crew. Jim introduced the men as either wranglers for the stock or stuntmen who doubled as extras.

With the promised cold drinks in their hands, Brandy and Karen accepted the bale of hay offered as a seat by one of the men. No such deference was shown to Jim, and he seemed not to expect it as he leaned a shoulder against the building only a foot or two from where Brandy and Karen were sitting.

The conversation didn't slacken when they joined the group, but continued in the same light vein as before. The talk mainly consisted of swapping stories of other location films they had been on and the things that had gone wrong, sometimes hilarious and sometimes dangerous.

The men didn't seem to object to being interrupted by questions from Brandy and Karen. In fact, they seemed to enjoy their audience. Brandy knew she could have sat for hours listening to their escapades.

One man clapped his hands on his thighs and pushed himself upright from a squatting position. "Well," he breathed in, "I guess they aren't going to need me today. They oughta be wrappin' things up about now, I would say, because the light's going."

Brandy glanced at the hands on her watch. Nearly six. It seemed impossible that more than four hours could have passed since she and Karen had arrived at the gate, but the lengthening shadows confirmed the hour. Quickly she stood up, instinctively brushing away the wisps of hay that stuck to her tan slacks.

"It's time we were leaving, too," she told Karen.

"I suppose you're right," Karen sighed, and straightened from the bale with obvious reluctance.

The rest of the group started dispersing as Jim stepped forward. Brandy smiled at him, aware of how much she had enjoyed the entire afternoon. He studied her with quiet thoughtfulness.

"Thank you for showing us around." Brandy didn't know what else to do, so she offered him her hand.

The gesture brought a twitching hint of a smile to his mouth as he accepted her hand with mock solemnness. "I hope you enjoyed it. I'm just sorry you feel you have to leave so soon."

"It's late." Her stomach was reacting crazily to the firm grip of his hand as he held hers longer than was politely required.

"Yes, it is," Karen said as though she hated to admit that fact, "and by the time I drive Brandy home and get back to my apartment, it's going to be even later yet. I've enjoyed it all tremendously, Mr. Corbett. I can't thank you enough for asking us to come."

"There's no need to thank me," he denied

smoothly. "And I would prefer that you call me Jim."

"Yes ... all right, Jim." A pleased smile beamed from Karen's face at the friendly offer.

His attention shifted to Brandy, and he ran a measuring eye over the honey-gold curls and the turned-up tip of her nose. "Didn't you drive your car today?"

"No," she shook her head, "Dad's using it. Mom was going to need their car to go to some meeting or other after classes, so Dad borrowed mine to drive to Phoenix this afternoon."

"Then there's no need for you to drive so far out of your way, Karen, to take Brandy home. I'll give her a ride," he stated.

"Oh, no—" Brandy started to protest, not wanting him to think she had been angling for an invitation.

"Accepted," Karen declared, blithely interrupting. "But—"

"But what, Brandy?" Jim openly mocked her attempts to argue. "Your house isn't out of my way and I'm willing to take you, so why object?"

Brandy struggled for a delicate explanation. "I just don't want you to think—"

"I know what you don't want me to think," he interrupted dryly. "If you're ready to leave, we'll go and get my car. It's in the private lot."

Brandy hesitated an instant longer, then nodded agreement. She couldn't seem to control the ambivalent sensations she felt toward him. She wanted his company, his attention, and with equal determina-

123

tion, she wanted to avoid him. She felt like a child who threw away a toy, then wanted it back.

"If that's all settled," Karen said gaily, "then I'm off for home. See you tomorrow, Brandy, and thanks again for the tour, Jim."

With a cheery wave, she was walking away toward the main gate. Out of the corner of her eye, Brandy glanced at Jim who was regarding her so silently. She was not going to appear childish or make a fool of herself again by trying to refuse his invitation. She couldn't forget who he was, but if Jim Corbett wanted to give her a ride home, she was going to take it. The decision didn't lessen the jumping of her nerves.

"Shall we go?" Brandy suggested with a determined lift of her chin.

With a mocking inclination of his head, Jim agreed, his hand lightly closing over her elbow to guide her in the right direction.

The absence of the buffering presence of Karen made Brandy feel awkward and self-conscious. Her lighthearted friend had made conversation flow easily; now she couldn't think of a thing to say that wouldn't sound forced and artificial.

Various members of the film crew waved to them as they left. All of them seemed to regard Brandy's accompaniment as natural; they didn't seem concerned that it was she and not the raven-haired actress that Jim was escorting.

Now that Brandy was alone with Jim, she wondered again whether he was using her to keep the obviously possessive LaRaine Evans in line. All the gossip had indicated that their relationship was on a very intimate level. Yet Jim had been cool toward the actress, antagonistic at times.

It was all too confusing. She was out of her league. She was used to straightforward, undisturbing relationships with men, yet every time she was with Jim Corbett, she felt bewildered and pulled in two different directions at the same time. Never before in her life had she felt inferior or incapable of handling a situation, but she did now.

"Why the frown?" His dark head was tipped to the side as he opened the passenger door of the Mark V.

Immediately it smoothed itself away. "Was I frowning?" She shrugged, and then quickly slid on to the contoured leather seat. "I was just thinking—about nothing really important."

He made no comment as he closed her door and walked around to the driver's side. The powerful engine sprang immediately to life at the turn of the key. He reversed the car out of the parking stall and turned it toward the parking lot exit.

"Are you still worrying, Brandy?" Jim asked quietly, flicking her a brief glance while he waited for a break in the traffic before pulling on to the road.

"Worrying?" she stalled. "I don't know what you mean."

"Isn't your inferiority complex troubling you for allowing James Corbett to take you home?" There was a deepening of the groove on one side of his mouth.

"I don't feel inferior to you, Jim," Brandy corrected softly.

"That was the impression you gave me when you turned down my dinner invitation," he replied, as the car accelerated on to the road.

"I don't feel inferior to you," she repeated, "it's just that we're two totally different types. Your world isn't like mine at all!"

"You saw a part of my world today and met some of the people I work with. Did you find them so extraordinary that you couldn't be friendly toward them? Were they so very different from yourself and the people you know?"

Brandy felt trapped. "No," she admitted grudgingly.

"Then why don't you reconsider your decision?"

"Which decision?" she countered.

"The one about having dinner with me," he answered smoothly.

Brandy wanted to take back her refusal. She wanted to say yes to Jim this time. But the words of acceptance lodged in her throat. She had been so adamant before. Rather than say anything she stared out the window, hating the wall of pride she had erected.

Jim let the silence stand, not prodding her for any kind of reply. Slowing the car, he turned it into a side road and switched off the motor. Her heart thudded against her ribs as she darted him a wary glance.

"Why are we stopping here?" She looked around to see if there was a legitimate reason for their stop.

"It's a good, quiet place to walk." He opened the door and stepped out. Leaning down, his gaze challenged her. "Are you coming?"

Surprised by the unexpected change of circumstances, Brandy faltered, "But ... my parents will be expecting me home. I'm usually there to fix dinner in the evenings."

A sardonically amused light entered his dark eyes. "I wasn't suggesting that we spend the night, only go for a short walk. You're a grown woman—I doubt that your parents will worry if you're a couple of hours late. As for dinner, I'm sure your mother can manage to cope."

His reasoning wasn't to be argued with, so Brandy surrendered to the inevitable and stepped out of the car. He waited until she had walked around to join him before starting out.

Heat radiated from the sun-baked desert floor, although the intensity of the sun was on the wane. The scattered forest of giant saguaro cactus rose to dwarf them as they made their way around the sage-brush and prickly pear.

The tops of the rounded ends of the saguaro trunk and its arms were crowned with a waxlike blossom, the state flower of Arizona. The saguaro and the organ pipe were always the last cactus to bloom, and because they were the largest, they kindly let their smaller cousins be the first to herald spring.

In March, the little hedgehog cactus would open its rose-purple cups, and a month later the spiny ocotillo would release its scarlet-flamed trumpets. But the giants waited until late May, with the first saguaro blossom signaling the beginning of the Papago Indian's New Year.

Walking among these ancient towering plants with their vertical ridges of thorns, Brandy felt her gaze pulled repeatedly to the majestic saguaros. Their trunks stretched upward to the sky, a multitude of arms branching out and raised boldly to the sun. Their endurance in a hostile climate was marked by the fact that a saguaro was seventy-five years old before it began to branch out.

Most of the cacti surrounding Brandy and Jim now were older than the statehood of Arizona. Some of them were nearer the age of the United States. The timeless magic of them enfolded her.

"The tales they could tell!" Brandy murmured.

Jim glanced down, an indulgent gleam in his eyes. "I take it you don't regret coming for a walk."

"I don't regret it." She darted a quick look at his amused expression. "I didn't really object in the first place," she defended.

"Didn't you?" A dark eyebrow arched to doubt her word.

"Well, only a little bit," she admitted as a self-mocking smile curved his lips.

A car hummed along the road behind them, an unwanted reminder of civilization. Brandy much preferred to have her thoughts dwell on the natural beauty around her.

"Let's walk a little farther," Jim suggested, taking her arm and walking at a leisurely pace that kept her by his side.

"You know, I'm never able to understand why some people don't like the desert," she commented idly. "Even Karen says it's harsh and ugly and barren."

"It's a case of different likes, I suppose," Jim answered idly.

"Do you like the desert?" His answer was suddenly important to her. She didn't think she could stand it if he didn't see the beauty in it that she did.

"Yes," was his clear, simple reply.

"I don't think I'd ever want to live any place else," Brandy declared, looking over the landscape that had always been part of her home. There was a haze of lavender on the edge of the western horizon.

"Neither would I."

She glanced at him in surprise. "But you don't live here?"

"Yes, I do," he smiled. "I have for years, but it's been one of my few well-kept secrets."

"Where?" she demanded in a still doubting voice. "You don't mean around here?"

"If you say I don't, then I don't," he shrugged, taunting her with his smile.

Stopping, she gazed at him, realizing that he was telling her the truth. "You are serious, aren't you?" she said. "You do live in Arizona."

"Yes," Jim nodded.

129

"You don't have to tell me where," Brandy added hastily. If it wasn't common knowledge, then he obviously wanted his home kept secret. Although eaten up with curiosity, she didn't want to force him to disclose the actual location.

"I don't mind telling you. I don't think you'll spread it around, knowing how much I value my privacy." But he held her expectant look for long seconds without satisfying her curiosity. "My home is the Saguaro ranch."

Her turquoise eyes widened with shock. "But that's owned by a corporation in California," she protested. "It has been for years."

"That's right," Jim agreed smoothly. "I simply happen to be the sole stockholder of the corporation."

"I don't know what to say," she laughed shortly, believing him yet finding it incredible.

"How about, hi neighbor?"

A wide smile dimpled her cheeks as she held out her hand. "Hi, neighbor." After a brisk handshake, he retained possession of her hand, but Brandy was still too bemused by the sudden turn of events to notice. "How do you manage it? I mean, how could you keep it a secret?"

"There's a small airstrip on the ranch that I fly in and out of so my visits are never known about by the public," he answered.

"But the men on the ranch know, the ones that work for you," she pointed out.

130

"Yes, but then I pay their salaries, don't I?" Jim mocked. "Part of what I pay them for is to keep quiet."

"They've done an excellent job." Brandy shook her head.

"Oh, there have been one or two slips that started a circle of questions," he admitted, "but the denials were always eventually believed."

"Isn't anyone suspicious about you staying there now?" She tipped her head curiously to one side.

"Were you?" Jim countered.

With a laughing smile, she answered her own question. "I assumed that you were invited to stay there while you were filming the movie by whoever owned the ranch."

"That's what everyone believes. And of course, it's true, since I did invite myself to stay there." Laughter danced wickedly in his eyes.

With a small, amazed shake of her head, Brandy lowered her gaze, absently focusing on the large hand that held hers. "You've been my neighbor all this time," she mused, a half-smile still on her lips.

The pressure of his hand increased slightly, drawing her serene, jewel-colored eyes back to his face. The unfathomable darkness of his eyes seemed to pull her into their depths.

The fluttering in her chest took away her breath as she seemed to float into his arms, always a captive of those compelling eyes. Tilting her head back, Brandy watched them draw nearer, their warmth burning her.

Then her gaze slid to his descending mouth.

As it closed possessively over hers, her lashes, fluttered down in a golden veil over her cheeks. There was nothing exploratory or tender in his kiss, its fierceness demanding that she respond.

The moaning sigh that slipped from her throat released the last of her inhibitions as she wound her arms tightly around his neck. Her flesh was pliant to the molding caress of his hands that sent strange new sensations shooting through her limbs.

The world became a perpetual sundown. The colors in her mind were ten times more brilliant, painted by a heavenly hand. It was a scattered rainbow of reds and orange, the vivid spectrum ranging from coppery gold to scarlet to magenta, cerise and lavender.

Crushed against him as she was, Jim's male outline was forever imprinted on her flesh. The sensuous touch of his lips along her neck and the hollow of her throat evoked more fiery sensations that rocked her slender body with their explosive effects. Then he was withdrawing from her, not loosening the hard embrace that kept her pressed against him. His dark head was drawn back, the challenging glitter of his gaze studying the protesting plea of her expression.

"Tell me again that you won't have dinner with me," he dared in a husky, threatening tone.

Her gold head moved bewilderedly to the side, wondering how he could think she would refuse after the way she had surrendered so completely to him.

She opened her mouth. "I—"

He covered it immediately in a punishing kiss that robbed the strength from her legs until she was clinging weakly to him for support. Then rough kisses were rained over her eyes, nose, cheeks and ear.

"I'm not going to let you go until you say yes," he warned thickly, his mouth moving against the lobe of her ear.

"Then," Brandy swallowed to steady the throb of ecstasy in her voice, "I'll wait a while," she whispered, turning her head to find his lips.

"You witch!" He laughed shortly, but with triumph gave her the kiss she sought and drew away before she was satisfied. He stared silently at the soft light that radiated from her face, his reaction to the burning embrace not as transparent as hers. His chest heaved in a deep breath against her. "I think we'd better go back to the car before you start something you might regret."

At this moment, Brandy was certain she would not regret anything that might happen, not anything, but she checked the impulse to wind her arms tighter around his neck. When his hands slid to her elbows, she reluctantly let her arms be pulled away.

Brandy was half afraid that he was going to withdraw invisibly from her the way he had done that morning on the desert after the sandstorm. She didn't think she could endure it if he asked her to forget about this kiss, too.

But instead of stepping away, leaving her trembling and alone, Jim wrapped an arm around her shoulder and drew her to his side, protectively nestled against his shoulder. Matching his step to her smaller stride, he started toward the road.

In the car, Jim didn't start the motor. He turned sideways in the seat, his arm resting along the back cushion. His powerfully carved and bronzed features were drawn in lines of serious contemplation.

"Success or fame doesn't change a man, Brandy," he stated quietly. "He remains essentially what he always was. His faults or weaknesses are simply magnified tenfold, whether it's vanity, selfishness, conceit or cruelty. The same is true of whatever good points he possessed. The man doesn't change. The only thing that does change is the way the others, friends and strangers, look at him." His eyes seemed to pierce into her innermost soul. "Do you understand what I'm saying?"

With an amazing calm, Brandy returned his intensely penetrating gaze. A wondrous warmth filled her heart as she realized what he was telling her. The joy of the knowledge shimmered in her blue-green eyes.

"Yes, you're saying that you are the man I met on the desert. That you were never anything else," she answered quietly. "I changed you into someone else in my mind."

He released his breath in a slow sigh, a devastating smile curving the hard line of his mouth. Her pulse raced at the sight of it, sensuously male and disturbingly warm.

"I, Jim Corbett, would like to hear you say again that you'll have dinner with me on Saturday night." The firm, caressing voice sent shivers dancing down her spine.

"I would love to have dinner with you on Saturday night." Her voice vibrated with husky overtones that were emotion-charged.

"I'm not going to let you change your mind, you know that, don't you?" he stated. "I'll kidnap you if I have to." His mouth quirked to make a joke out of what was essentially an unhumorous threat.

"Promise?" Brandy smiled impishly.

Wickedly playful lights glinted in his eyes as Jim faced the front of the car. "Just try me," he murmured, and turned the key in the ignition.

Brandy leaned back in her seat as he turned the car on to the road. An unbelievable mixture of blissful contentment and giddy excitement claimed her. She had fallen in love with Jim Corbett, and the admission didn't frighten her one bit.

Silently she gazed at him. His rugged masculine profile was vividly outlined by the crimson-orange colors of the setting sun. The formidable strength in his features was reassuring.

With a sideways glance, Jim intercepted her study of him. Without a word he reached out and took her hand, holding it gently in his all the way to her home.

In the driveway, he didn't shut off the motor, nor did he release her hand. His dark eyes surveyed her silently for a minute.

135

"Will seven-thirty be all right on Saturday?"

It seemed like such a long time till Saturday. "Yes, seven-thirty is fine," Brandy agreed.

Jim hesitated. "I may get held up. We'll be shooting on Saturday, so if I'm not here right on time, don't give up on me." His mouth quirked into a winning kind of half-smile to make his statement sound like less of an order.

"I'll wait." For an eternity if I have to, she added to herself.

"You'd better mean that, Brandy." For a brief second, the intensity of his low voice made her think she had spoken the thought aloud. "Because I'll be here. If I see that I'm going to be very late, I'll try to phone you."

"Okay," she nodded understandingly.

Reasured, his eyes darkened with an intimate fire. "Come here."

She didn't need a second invitation to move toward him, her lips parting willingly under the hard pressure of his. While her senses were still whirling from his heady kiss, Jim set her away.

"You'd better go in," he said, "before your parents decide to send out another search party for you."

"Yes, I'd better." But her shaking hands moved very slowly for the door handle.

As she opened it, Jim repeated, "Saturday at seven-thirty." As if she could forget.

CHAPTER SEVEN

THE HEADLIGHT BEAMS from a car turning into the driveway flashed on to the living-room window.

"He's here. Mom, do I look all right?" Brandy felt more nervous than she had been on her first date or any date since then. She looked from her mother's patiently smiling face to her reflection in the bronze-framed mirror.

Choosing what to wear had been an agonizing decision. She couldn't make up her mind whether to wear something chicly sophisticated or casually elegant. In the end, the outfit she chose fitted neither category.

The cream-white pants outfit in a thin, clinging knit and wide flared legs did show off her golden tan and molded her slender curves. The tunic-styled top was classically plain, the perfect background for the Navajo-designed squash-blossom necklace she wore. The turquoise stones almost exactly matched the blue-green shade of her eyes. Earrings in the same trumpet-shaped curls tucked behind her ear to show off the long curve of her neck.

"You look lovely," Lenora Ames assured her.

"I hope so." Brandy started as she heard a car door slam.

"Brandy." There was a thread of caution in her mother's voice.

A faint smile touched Brandy's mouth. She knew what her mother wanted to say: the veiled warnings that Jim was older, more experienced and accustomed to a different life-style, and mostly that he was a celebrity. She wanted to caution her not to become too deeply involved with him. Brandy knew all of that, and it didn't alter anything.

"I know what I'm doing, Mom," she insisted gently, a serenity taking hold of her at the certainty of her emotions.

But her composure went out of the window when the doorbell chimed. Her knees were quivering as she opened the front door, smiling tremulously at the tall man dressed in a dark suit with a deep charcoal-gray waistcoat of shimmering silk.

His gaze raked her form in slow appraisal, quickening the beat of her heart. The darkening glow of admiration in his eyes restored her confidence, and she reached for his hand to draw him inside the house.

"You're only a quarter of an hour late," she declared brightly, as if the minutes hadn't dragged.

His attention shifted to the glossy shimmer of her lips, his look almost a physical caress as his hand tightened around hers with unmistakable possession.

"You're beautiful," his deep voice murmured softly.

Inside with the door closed, the light of intimacy in his eyes held her a silent captive. Brandy wanted to lose herself in the midnight sky of his gaze. She forgot that they were not alone in the living room until her father coughed delicately. A faint pink becomingly blushed her cheeks as she withdrew her hand from Jim's unresisting hold. His features softened into a half-smile.

"I'll get my bag, then we can leave," Brandy murmured.

"No hurry," Jim drawled lazily, moving farther into the room toward her parents. "It's good to see you again." He held out a hand to her father.

There was a polite and friendly exchange of greetings while Brandy collected her bag, then walked with quiet pride to her place at Jim's side.

He glanced down, his eyes moving warmly over her glowing face. "Ready?"

"Yes," she nodded. "Goodnight, Mom, Dad."

His hand slipped lightly to the inside of her elbow. "Goodnight." The wish was offered jointly to her parents. Then he added perceptively, "Don't worry, Mrs. Ames. Brandy is quite safe with me."

Her mother smiled in surprise and looked curiously at Brandy, but didn't comment. In the next instant, the pressure of his hand was guiding Brandy towards the door.

Outside, she tipped her head sideways, an earring trailing along the side of her neck. "How did you know my mother was concerned about me going out with you?"

"It's normal," Jim smiled mockingly down at her. "Among other things, I'm certain my reputation has preceded me."

"True," she agreed with a jesting light in her eyes to match his. "I've heard that you make a habit of loving them and leaving them."

"Worried?" He held the car door for her.

"Not yet," she laughed, but it was strangely true.

Before she could slide into the car, his hand caught her arm to hold her motionless. Surprised, she looked at him with questioning eyes. A finger lifted her chin as he smiled and warmly kissed her parted lips.

"Don't worry," he ordered, and lightly pushed her into the car.

What did that mean? Brandy watched him walk around the car. Was he telling her that this time it would be different? She was too eager to enjoy every minute spent in his company to use any of the precious time trying to guess what was going through his mind.

"Are you hungry?" Jim reversed the car out of the drive and turned on to the gravel road toward the city of Tucson.

"Starved!" Brandy declared fervently. "Where are we going?"

He named a restaurant that she was familiar with although she hadn't been there. When she didn't comment, he asked, "Is there something wrong?"

"No," she answered quickly. "I thought—" she hesitated, "I thought that we might eat at your ranch. I wasn't sure whether you would want to go anywhere public."

"Did you think I would be ashamed to be seen with

you?'' he accused, the dark slash of his brows drawn together in an exasperated frown.

"No, I thought you would want privacy," Brandy protested.

The frown was swept away by a quiet chuckle, the rapid transformation from controlled anger to humor confusing her with its swiftness.

"Why is that funny?"

"Becuse I convinced myself that you'd be reluctant to spend an evening alone with me in my home." Jim darted her a brief look, a roguish sparkle in his eyes. "The real truth is that I didn't trust myself to be alone with you."

A hot flaming weakness licked through her limbs at the prospect of Jim making love to her. The heady thought took her breath away.

"No reply?" he mocked with teasing humor.

Brandy bobbed her head negatively. "None," she said, not able to make her voice sound calm and unconcerned when her senses were in such a turmoil imagining what it might be like.

His voice immediately became very calm and gentle. "Does the idea frighten you, Brandy?"

"No," she breathed truthfully.

There was a surprised silence, then she saw the whistle flash of a rueful smile. "Wish you hadn't said that."

"Why?"

"Because I might take you at your word, literally." His gaze smoldered over her face, stopping her heart, then sending it rocketing off. "And it's too soon for you yet."

He was probably right, Brandy acknowledged silently. She wasn't used to the fact that she loved him yet. A few days ago she hadn't even wanted to see him again, probably because subconsciously she had known she would fall in love with him if she did.

They were driving through the mountain pass, the curve in the road giving them their first glimpse of Tucson. The lights of the city glimmered low in the purpling haze of sunset. The mountain ranges protecting the city were dark silhouettes against the sky-line.

"Have you been to this restaurant before?" Jim deftly changed the subject.

"No. Have you?"

"Yes. They're accustomed to having well-known personalities as customers, so we won't create a stir when we arrive," he assured her.

It was partially true, Brandy later discovered as they entered the restaurant. Jim was recognized instantly, although she was certain that even if he hadn't been a well-known actor, he still would have commanded attention.

The maître d'hotel stepped forward. "Mr. Corbett, this is indeed an honor," he said with a deferential nod of his head.

Jim acknowledged the comment with a faint smile. "A quiet table for two, please." With emphasis on the "quiet."

"Of course, sir."

Within a few minutes they were led to a fairly secluded corner of the room. It was impossible for Brandy not to be aware of the heads turning as they walked by the tables of people. It was a silent recognition to Jim, unlike the camera clicking, autograph response to his presence that had occurred at the movie location of Old Tucson. She realized that was what he meant when he had said their arrival wouldn't create a stir in this restaurant, but he was definitely the object of considerable attention.

She wasn't conscious of being studied with almost equal interest. Not simply because she was being escorted by Jim Corbett or envied because his arm rested so possessively along the back of her waist.

As a couple they made a stunning contrast. Jim was tall and broad-shouldered and utterly masculine, while Brandy was deceptively shorter next to him, slenderly curved and essentially feminine. Her classically simple cream white pant suit and her fair coloring were set off by the darkness of his hair and eyes, and the richly tailored dark suit he wore.

At the table, Jim stepped ahead of Brandy to hold out a chair for her. When she sat down, he leaned forward as if to edge her chair closer to the table. Instead he warmly pressed his mouth against the pulsing cord of her neck, sending goosebumps over her arms.

Disconcerted by his action, she glanced around the room, catching the knowing looks of those who had seen the intimate caress. She tried to laugh away the hint of pink in her cheeks as Jim sat beside her.

"You shouldn't have done that. You made all your female fans jealous."

"And all the men envious," he countered, lazily surveying her self-conscious expression.

"Don't be silly." Brandy opened the menu to escape his disturbing gaze.

"I'm not," Jim replied smoothly. "I saw the looks you received when we walked through. There isn't a man in the house who wouldn't want to trade places with me. Now they know they have to go through me to get to you."

She gave him a startled glance, but he was studying the menu. She wasn't able to tell by the impassive expression on his carved features whether he was serious or merely being gallant.

"I imagine they thought that since I was with you, I was someone they should recognize and they were trying to place me," she tried to shrug away his compliment, if that was what it was.

"Possibly," Jim admitted, his dark gaze dancing over her, "but that wasn't all they were thinking."

The waiter appeared at their table. "Would you like cocktails before ordering?"

His arrival successfully changed the subject. With cocktails ordered, Jim leaned back in his chair, unconsciously flexing a shoulder muscle. The action prompted Brandy to notice the faint lines of tiredness around his mouth.

144

"Did you have a rough day?" Her softly worded question was gently sympathetic.

"Does it show?" His mouth crooked wryly, then he sighed. "It was a physical day, running up and down stairs, busting down doors, rolling in the dirt, discovering muscles I'd forgotten." He laughed quietly at himself. "Just your average, ordinary day at the office."

"That's what it sounds like," Brandy agreed with a dimpling smile. "It also sounds as if you aren't in very good condition," she teased.

"I'm getting old," Jim shrugged without a note of regret in his low voice.

The waiter returned with their drinks. Brandy waited until he had left before she responded to Jim's statement.

"You must be ancient. What are you—all of thirty-three?"

"You haven't read my resumé or you'd know I'm thirty-four," he corrected.

'Jim, darling!" The throaty female voice struck Brandy like a body blow to her midsection.

Her widened, blue-green eyes swerved to the raven-haired LaRaine Evans gliding toward their table. A stunning gown of black lace left little of the actress's figure to the imagination, the color intensifying the midnight blackness of her hair and eyes, the vivid red of her lips and her ivory complexion. Brandy felt like a pale nothing in comparison.

A quick glance at Jim found him rising to his feet,

his expression unrevealing, and she couldn't tell if he was surprised, glad, or annoyed by the brunette's appearance.

Without regard to the onlooking restaurant customers, or perhaps because of the audience, LaRaine moved directly to Jim, spreading ringed fingers on his chest and rising up to kiss his smoothly-shaven cheek. A red brand was left on his tanned skin.

"Look what I've done," LaRaine murmured, her dark eyes sparkling in satisfaction at the scarlet mark. She reached into his pocket and removed his handkerchief, dabbing at the mark with the familiarity of a wife—or a mistress. Brandy's stomach churned at the sight. "There, darling," the brunette purred, "it's all gone now."

When she started to replace the white kerchief in his pocket, Jim took it from her hand and put it away himself. "Thank you, LaRaine," he offered dryly.

There was a sensuously petulant droop of her lower lip. "I'm quite angry with you, darling, for running off like that tonight without a word."

"I was late for an engagement," Jim answered smoothly. "You remember Miss Ames, don't you?" forcing LaRaine to direct her attention to Brandy.

Cool, faintly haughty brown eyes looked at Brandy. "Of course, I do," the actress drawled. "Brandy, isn't it? I remember it was such an unusual name."

The comment left the impression that if it hadn't been for the name LaRaine would have forgotten having met her entirely.

146

"That's correct, Miss Evans," replied Brandy.

"Do call me LaRaine," she insisted, and looked pointedly at Jim. "After all, we do have so much in common."

Meaning we both want the same man, Brandy thought with a sinking feeling in her stomach. At this moment, she felt miserably inadequate to compete with the likes of LaRaine Evans for Jim's attention.

"As for you, Jim," LaRaine smiled bewitchingly, "I'll forgive you for not taking the time to let me know you were coming tonight. I know you like to be punctual when you tell a girl you'll pick her up at a certain time. Since you did come to my party after all, I won't scold you for all I went through wondering if you'd come or not."

Brandy looked warily at Jim, questions racing through her mind. What was LaRaine talking about? What was all this about a party? Jim hadn't mentioned anything about it.

"Was your party this evening, LaRaine?" He tilted his head, aloof and cool. "I do remember you mentioning it, but I'm afraid I'd forgotten about it."

"Now you're being cruel, darling," the actress declared. The secret smile on her face seemed to say that she knew why and understood. "You know very well that I told you we all would be meeting here tonight."

The statement caused a painful picture to form in Brandy's mind. If Jim had no intention of joining the party and had brought her here anyway, it could have

147

been for only one reason—he had wanted LaRaine to see him with Brandy. She couldn't believe it was all a coincidence.

"The others are in the lounge," LaRaine continued. "Why don't you bring your drink and come and join us? And you, too, Brandy."

"No, thank you," Jim refused smoothly. "I think Brandy and I would prefer to have a quiet dinner alone."

"Nonsense!" A practised, throaty laugh was emitted from the perfectly outlined red mouth. "Every girl would prefer a party. Isn't that right, Brandy?"

What was she supposed to say? She looked to Jim for an answer, but he was lazily studying the dark-haired beauty standing so very near his side. They were such a perfect pair, each so dark and compelling in their looks. Was she supposed to be persuaded to join the party or refuse? She didn't want to be drawn into their argument—whatever it was. It hurt to think that Jim was using her this way. It hurt unbearably.

Feeling betrayed by the way he had misled her into believing that he had genuinely wanted her company only tonight, Brandy refused to answer LaRaine's question in any positive way.

"Not necessarily," she hedged, glancing briefly to Jim.

"Of course you would, a young girl like you." La-Raine waved aside her response. The slender wing of an eyebrow was lifted in sarcastic mockery as the brunette glanced at Jim through her long lashes. "I do

148

believe she's afraid of you, darling. She doesn't want to say the wrong thing for fear you'll be angry."

A black frown clouded his features as he shot Brandy a stormy look. "Do you want to go to the party?" he demanded with ominous quiet.

No, she wanted to scream, I want to stay here and have dinner with you alone. But how could she say that? Surely it was already obvious that was what she wanted.

"It doesn't matter to me," she shrugged, and looked away, feeling angry, hurt and confused all at the same time.

"There, you see, she does want to come!" LaRaine declared triumphantly. "She's simply too shy to tell you so!"

His mouth thinned into an uncompromising line, his jaw clenched tautly. "In that case, we'll join your party, LaRaine. Lead the way." His hand closed over the back of Brandy's chair. Only she could feel the controlled violence in his seemingly polite assistance.

The look on the brunette's face was one of feline satisfaction as she led them toward the lounge. Jim's hand almost punishingly clasped Brandy's elbow. He paused once to tell the waiter they were joining some friends, forcing Brandy to do the same. The delay put LaRaine several steps ahead of them.

"There was no need to be hesitant about joining the party." Jim's voice growled near Brandy's ear. "You should have said so instead of hinting."

His unwarranted accusation prompted Brandy to retaliate. "If I'd wanted to go, I would have said so. But it was obvious that it was what you wanted!"

"What *I* wanted?" Jim glared.

"It's why we came here, isn't it?" She tossed her head back and stared straight ahead, the dangling earrings bouncing against her neck.

He laughed softly, the black temper vanishing as quickly as it had come. "I should have remembered that you have no qualms about speaking your mind, but now we're committed."

She tipped her head back to look at him. "Do you mean you didn't want to?"

"No," he said quite firmly, but the grooves around his mouth deepened. "I would have been content to have a quiet dinner with you."

They had entered the lounge. The bombardment of greetings from the party members prevented Brandy from asking Jim to enlarge on that statement. If his intention in taking her out was to make LaRaine jealous, he would hardly be willing to tell her that. Not when he must know that at the very least she was infatuated with him.

There were approximately ten people in the party group, not counting Brandy and Jim. The exact number was uncertain because some were on the dance floor, floating around changing partners, and one or two were dashing back and forth to the bar to get quick refills of their drinks.

One thing Brandy recognized instantly was that there were more men than women. The women who

150

were there were attractive in a plain sort of way; it was not surprising under the circumstances, Brandy decided. She doubted that LaRaine would want any genuine competition around her by choice. The actress's ego was probably also the reason more men were invited, so that she could be certain more than one would be flocking around her.

None of the people were among those Brandy had met at the movie location. Those who noticed her now as LaRaine briefly made the introductions regarded her curiously. Their looks were already accompanied by questioning glances from Jim to LaRaine. Whatever had been going on between the two of them must have been common knowledge to them.

Brandy felt decidedly uncomfortable. The artificial gaiety that bubbled around her was grating in its effusiveness. She was glad of the firm grip that kept her at Jim's side, despite LaRaine's less than subtle attempts to separate them.

Although Brandy was seated beside Jim, LaRaine occupied the chair to his right, her hand resting casually on his arm. The talk, led by LaRaine, centered on the day's filming, a subject that Brandy knew nothing about. There was little she could do except to listen so that possibly she might be able to join the conversation later.

One of the apparently unattached men sat down in the vacant chair beside her. He was comparatively young, only two or three years older than herself, with sandy hair streaked platinum by the sun.

"Hello." Despite the friendly smile that accompanied his greeting there seemed to be a perpetual gleam of rebellion in his blue eyes, a pale shade unlike the brilliant color of hers.

"Hello." Brandy knew she had been introduced to him, but his name escaped her.

"Bryce Conover is the name," he replied wryly, interpreting the blank look in her expression. "And you're Brandy."

She smiled an apology, then glanced at Jim to see if he had noticed the man at her side, but his dark head was tilted toward LaRaine, listening intently to what she was saying.

"I know you don't remember me," Bryce Conover's tenor voice was low, meant only for Brandy's ears, "but I noticed you when you came out to the set the other day with Jim."

"I'm sorry. There were so many people," Brandy shrugged. She felt suddenly cut adrift.

It was true that Jim had kept her by his side as though that was where he wanted her to be, and he had indicated that he hadn't wanted to join this party. Yet there he was talking to LaRaine—he was virtually ignoring her now.

"That's all right. I understand," Bryce replied. The trace of bitterness in his voice said he was accustomed to being overlooked, but didn't like it. A slow tune was playing softly in the background. "Would you like to dance?"

A refusal formed on her lips, then a sliding look

saw the long scarlet fingernails curling possessively on Jim's wrist and the seductive light in LaRaine's dark eyes as she gazed into his face, the hard mouth curved slightly in an answering smile. In painful acknowledgment, Brandy doubted if Jim would even notice she was gone.

"Yes," she accepted firmly. A determined smile was given to Bryce as she rose to her feet, aware of Jim's sideways glance of frowning surprise.

"I asked Brandy to dance," Bryce informed him. "You don't mind, do you, Jim?" The question was coolly offhand with a suggestion of challenge. His arm curved around Brandy's shoulders.

"Of course he doesn't," LaRaine answered before Jim had a chance.

Bryce Conover didn't wait for a further answer as he turned Brandy toward the small dance floor. Reluctantly, she moved into her partner's arms, resisting his efforts to mold her close to him. Her gaze strayed to the table and Jim.

"You might as well forget about him." Bryce's pale blue eyes arrogantly met her guilty start. "Corbett is all staked out as LaRaine's property."

"Really?" Brandy tried to sound coolly indifferent. "Does he know that?"

A mocking smile was her answer. "Everyone knows the two of them are skirmishing now. That's the way it always goes when you have two strong personalities. The outcome is obvious—Corbett will come out on top. But they have to go through this stage. It always happens. It's like a courtship ritual."

Brandy's skin went cold. "I see," she said stiffly. "And what is my role in all this?"

"You're the fair-haired ingénue, a striking contrast to LaRaine's more earthy attraction. Regardless of what you've seen in the movies, the ingénue rarely ends up in the hero's arms in real life." His head bent toward hers. Brandy turned, but not swiftly enough to avoid the caress of his lips against her cheek. "You're being used, honey, to bring LaRaine up to scratch."

His statement vocalized the doubt that had been plaguing her since LaRaine had appeared. She didn't want to believe it, but the ugly facts were staring her in the face. What other conclusion could there be?

The music ended and Brandy pushed herself out of Bryce's arms. His hand snaked out to claim her waist, but she jerked it away.

"There's another song starting. Let's dance, honey." His sandy head bobbed toward their table. "They don't want you there."

Her turquoise eyes flashed shimmering green toward the table. From this angle, Brandy could see LaRaine leaning sideways in her chair toward Jim. His granite features revealed nothing. If he found the glistening red mouth alluring, he didn't show it.

LaRaine's half-turned position exposed more shadowy cleavage where the plunging neckline gaped open. Brandy wanted to rush over and stuff a handkerchief down the front of the black lace gown, but it wouldn't have concealed the actress's voluptuous figure, and the

154

impulse died before she was tempted to act.

A wounded anger drove Brandy back to the table. All of her doubts might be true, but she wasn't going to hide in a hole or on some dance floor like a whipped animal. Bryce followed, his displeasure obvious.

"You're a fool, Brandy," Bryce muttered as they drew near the table. "She'll tear you apart."

At their approach, Jim's gaze swerved to them, his eyes impenetrably hard like the rest of his features, flicking from one to the other with the smarting sting of a whip. Brandy became aware of Bryce's arm curving smoothly around her waist and the admiring expression that was on his face despite his last cutting remark. Yet Jim appeared coolly indifferent to the marked attention she was receiving from her new partner. Maybe he was relieved to have her off his hands.

Before Brandy could reach her chair at Jim's side, a man crossed her path, dark-suited with a smoothly polished appearance. He stopped beside Jim, blocking her from the chair. Brandy paused, waiting for an opportunity to claim her place at the table.

"Good evening, Mr. Corbett," the man clasped the back of Jim's shoulder in greeting, then glanced to LaRaine. "Miss Evans."

"Mr. Spencer, this is a surprise," Jim replied in a contradictingly dry voice that said it was not a surprise.

Bryce whispered in Brandy's ear. "He's a newspaper columnist."

The man glanced around the table at the fairly large gathering. "It looks as if you're having a celebration of some sort. Is someone engaged?" The probing question was directed to LaRaine's feline smile of satisfaction.

"Heavens, no, Mr. Spencer!" Her laughing protest that the question was ridiculous only made it sound the opposite. "It's merely a little weekend fling—if to celebrate anything, then the fact we don't have to work tomorrow."

"How disappointing," the columnist shook his head in mock regret. "I thought I might finally hear the two of you admit that things were serious between you."

"You have to remember, Spencer," Jim picked up his glass to study the liquor whirling inside, "we're working on the same picture. It's natural for us to be seen together. We're friends and fellow members of the profession." A dark, measuring look was directed at the columnist, almost daring him to dispute the simple statement of explanation to imply that there was anything more.

"That's right," LaRaine agreed huskily, a falsely demure look on her face. "Jim and I are just good friends."

"I'll quote you on that," the man laughed smugly.

A pain like cold steel plunged into Brandy's heart. She knew that the standard answer of "just good friends" meant the relationship was much more intimate. She watched in sickening anguish as the man walked away from the table. A muscle twitched in repressed anger alongside the powerful jaw when Jim met her tortured look.

As quickly as she could, she tried to conceal the hurt caused by her discovery. Had there been a choice, she would have sat anywhere other than beside Jim, but Bryce was already holding out the chair for her. With a defensively proud lift of her chin, she sat down.

Without a word of inquiry as to the wishes of the others, Jim signaled the waiter and asked him to prepare a table for them in the dining room. Brandy silently applauded his decision. She wanted the evening over with quickly.

A few offered a token protest, but not LaRaine. She was much too anxious to be on his side to oppose his decision.

CHAPTER EIGHT

LaRaine had supervised the seating arrangements at the circular dining table, ordering Brandy to sit beside Jim, a move that surprised Brandy until she realized that LaRaine had saved the coveted seat to his right for herself.

Conversation was again dominated by LaRaine, although twice Jim did try to encourage Brandy to join in. But as the meal progressed she grew quieter and quieter, the turned-up tip of her nose unconsciously elevating with pride.

When everyone was through eating, they lingered at the table over coffee. As the waiter came around to refill their cups a second time, Brandy wondered how much longer the evening was going to drag on. A tiny sigh broke from her lips.

The sound drew Jim's sharp gaze to her downcast face. Abruptly he refused more coffee and pushed his chair away from the table. An astonished blink later, he was drawing her chair away from the table.

"It's time we left, Brandy," he answered the unspoken query in her expression.

"So soon?" LaRaine protested with mock petulance, but otherwise unperturbed by his announcement. "The night is young."

"The night may be, but I'm not. And it's been a

long day," was his smooth reply, uttered very firmly.

After a round of goodnights to the other members of the party, Jim guided Brandy out of the restaurant to his car. The carved features gave no explanation for his mood of tight-lipped silence. Brandy reminded herself that she didn't care, and that she just wanted to get home the quickest way possible.

But it wasn't true. She did care. It didn't matter how crazy it was for her to have fallen in love with Jim Corbett. It wasn't something she could change in one evening, or maybe even a lifetime of evenings.

Soon they were speeding out of Tucson. Pride kept her silent as she stared out the window and tried not to remember how very well they had got along during the earlier part of the evening. That was before La-Raine appeared and raised the ugly probability that she was being used.

Without warning, Jim slowed the car on to the shoulder of the graveled road and switched off the motor. Brandy stiffened, self-consciously brushing a feathery-gold curl away from her temple.

"Why are we stopping here?" she asked curtly.

He turned slightly, leaning against his door, his arm resting across the steering wheel. The movement let the shadows of night close around to conceal his expression, but not his piercing gaze.

"I want to know what's the matter," he stated evenly.

She stared straight ahead. "I don't know what you're talking about."

"Something has happened to get your back up, and I want to know what it is."

She glanced at the bag in her lap, gleaming a ghost white in the pale moonlight. "You must be mistaken," she replied, trying to make her voice sound as cool and even as his.

"Your silence makes a louder denial," he mocked.

"My silence!" she laughed shortly and without humor. "You haven't said a word since before we left the restaurant." She hurled an accusing look of brilliant green at him.

"Considering the monosyllabic replies I received at dinner, I decided it was a waste of time until I could find out what was really bothering you." The dimness didn't lessen the watchful sensation of his dark eyes studying her. "I want to know why you're angry."

It was a command. Brandy pressed her lips together, wanting to vent all the anguished fury that had built inside her, yet unwilling to let Jim know that she had fallen in love with him.

"I'm not angry." The answer came out short and snappishly defensive.

With a swiftness she should have remembered, her chin was imprisoned by his hand as he roughly jerked her head around to face him. The moonlight bathed the demanding harshness of his features, black brows sternly lowering over his narrowing eyes. His closeness, the controlled anger glittering in his eyes, let her see that he meant exactly what he said.

"I want to know," he repeated with finality.

Part of her wanted to cower, but Brandy wasn't the type to knuckle under without putting up a fight. She let him hold her gaze without faltering, almost without flinching.

"A person doesn't like to be used any more than she likes to be laughed at," she replied in challenge.

A dark brow shot up. "Used?" Jim questioned arrogantly. "Is that what I'm supposed to be doing—using you?"

"Oh, please," she sighed in tight exasperation. Her fingers closed over the wrist of the hand that held her chin, but she couldn't push it away. "Spare me the protests of your innocence. Do you think I'm blind?"

"I'm beginning to wonder." His mouth thinned into a grim line. "How am I supposed to be using you?"

"Isn't it obvious?" she protested. Her lashes fluttered down to conceal the burst of pain that filled her eyes. "I know why you invited me out tonight, so there isn't any need to go on pretending."

"Why do you have to continue to talk in riddles? Why can't you say whatever it is in plain English?" His fingers tightened punishingly on her chin.

"I'm referring to LaRaine," Brandy flashed, "and that ridiculous charade of an evening."

He breathed in deeply, giving her a long, considering look before relaxing his hold on her chin. "I see," he drawled sardonically. "You've come to some conclusion about LaRaine and my motives for asking you out tonight."

She was not going to comment on that. "Would you please take me home?"

"I suppose you also think you're entitled to an explanation. I'm not giving you any," Jim declared coldly.

"I didn't ask for any, Mr. Corbett," she snapped.

There was a muttered imprecation simultaneously accompanied by a large hand circling her throat, the thumb forcing her chin upward. The hard force of his mouth closed bruisingly over hers.

Brandy fought his kiss for about five seconds before she let him overpower her resistance. An arm curled around her waist to drag her sideways from the seat and against the rock wall of his chest. There, her head was bent backward over his arm, her breath denied by the iron band of his arm crushing her against him.

The pain was sweet torture. As blackness swam before her closed eyes, she wound her arms around his shoulders, a hand slipping to the back of his neck to explore the luxuriant thickness of his dark hair growing down to the collar. The hard metal of her silver and turquoise necklace was digging into the soft flesh of her breasts.

Her mouth was released to breathe in the intoxicating air, scented with the sweet freshness of the desert and the musky aroma of his maleness. The hard, masculine lips roughly explored the arched curve of her throat.

Black fires blazed in his eyes as he lifted his head to

gaze into her face. Her thudding heart skipped quickly into a faster beat at the unmistakable desire that burned in his look.

As easily as one would maneuver a baby, Jim twisted her the rest of the way around and on to his lap. A hand slid in a sensuous caress along her hip and thigh. Cradled in his love-hold, she drew his head down to hers, lips parting at the touch of his.

The firm and passionate mastery of his mouth and the arousing touch of his hands over her body carried her to another plateau of sensations. She let Jim's expertise teach her what she didn't know until the willing pupil and the ardent teacher reached the last lesson.

With a broken sigh, Jim pulled his mouth away from her pliant lips and pressed her honey-gold head against the hollow of his shoulder. The erratic beat of his heart beneath her ear was in tune with the staccato rhythm of hers. The hand cupping her breast gently withdrew itself from beneath her tunic blouse, tenderly smoothing the rumpled material.

"Jim." Her whispering voice echoed the ache in her loins.

"Sssh!" His mouth moved against her hair in understanding as he held her closer. "Now do you understand why I didn't dare to be alone with you at the ranch?" he murmured.

Her lashes fluttered down. "Yes," she answered softly, almost with regret.

"In a car, there's time for second thoughts." She

felt the movement of his lips against her hair, the corners lifting into a smile.

"Second thoughts?" she repeated warily, wondering if he was sorry he had made love to her.

"Brandy." His soft chuckle moved the air about her face. "Are you always so uncertain of your attraction?"

"No." She tipped her head back to look at the rugged, compelling face so close to hers. She had never been uncertain before. "Only with you," she admitted hesitantly. She was still wary of letting him see how much power he had over her, yet it wasn't part of her nature to keep everything bottled up inside.

The suggestion of a smile faded from his mouth. His expression became thoughtfully serious, but its cause wasn't revealed by the enigmatic darkness of his eyes as he studied her face.

The grooves around his mouth deepened suddenly into a wry smile. "I'd better take you home."

Before Brandy could protest that she didn't want to leave yet, Jim was turning her off his lap and setting her again in the passenger seat.

After the car was started and he had turned it back on to the road, he took her hand and started talking, mostly about the film he was making and the crew. It was several minutes before Brandy realized he was explaining some of the things that had been discussed at the party that night, things that at the time she hadn't know about nor understood and had thus been subtly ostracized from the group. A wondrous flood of love warmed her heart at his understanding gesture.

In the driveway of her home, Jim shifted the gears into neutral, but left the motor running. The house was dark except for one light shining through the window near the front door.

"It isn't very late. Would you like to come in for some coffee?" Brandy offered.

"No," he refused, "I have a lot to do tomorrow, so I'd better have an early night."

"But you aren't working tomorrow," she frowned, remembering LaRaine's statement that they had tomorrow off.

"We aren't filming tomorrow," he corrected. "But I have a lot of script revisions to go over as well as a business meeting with Don, my manager. It will be a full day."

"Of course. I hadn't thought." She smiled weakly, trying to hide her disappointment. For the last couple of miles she had been hoping that Jim would want to spend part of tomorrow with her.

"Do you get up early in the morning?"

Brandy tipped her head curiously to one side. "Sometimes. Why?"

"I like to take a ride in the desert in the morning before the sun gets too hot. Would you like to come with me tomorrow?"

"Yes." She couldn't get her acceptance out fast enough.

"Is five-thirty too early?" he asked, adding, "I'll trailer my horse over here."

"That's fine," she agreed swiftly.

His firm mouth moved into a faint smile, and Jim leaned over and kissed her lips, his mouth moving warmly and mobilely over hers. Brandy still felt the disturbing pressure after he had moved away.

"In the morning," was his goodnight promise.

Shaken slightly, she nodded and stepped from the car. Jim waited in the driveway until she had unlocked the front door and stepped inside. Only when he had driven away did she realize that he had kept his word. He had said he would not explain about LaRaine, and he hadn't. She could not be any more certain about where she stood with him than she had been before. But at the moment nothing seemed able to trouble her greatly.

HUMMING MERRILY, Brandy filled the small glass with orange juice, taking a quick swallow, then turning to put the pitcher back in the refrigerator. There was a shuffle of footsteps in the hall.

"Brandy!" Her father paused in the doorway in the act of tying the sash of his robe. His pepper-gray hair was disheveled from sleep, his expression startled and disbelieving. "Lenora said she heard someone moving about."

He glanced out of the gray-darkened windows. "What are you doing up at this hour?"

"Jim's coming over. We're going for an early

166

morning ride." She set the juice pitcher in the refrigerator and walked to the counter. "He should be here any time now."

Stewart Ames frowned at the clock above the sink. "At five o'clock in the morning?"

"Look again, Dad." Brandy sipped hurriedly at her orange juice. "It's half-past five."

"The sky is barely light," he shrugged to indicate that a few minutes hardly made any difference.

The sound of an engine prompted Brandy to look out of the kitchen window. A pick-up truck hauling a horse trailer had stopped in the drive. She reached for the fringed leather jacket she had dropped over a kitchen chair.

"He's here now, Dad." Brandy pulled on her jacket. "The coffee is already made, all you and Mom have to do is plug it in to warm it up."

She started toward the side door, glad that she had already gone out and saddled her horse before grabbing a small breakfast. Her father's voice stopped her at the door.

"You know why it's called the crack of dawn, don't you, Brandy?" he asked in an offhand voice as he ran his fingers through his tousled hair.

"Why?" She tried not to sound impatient, but she really wasn't in the mood for any of his scientific explanations—not when Jim was waiting for her. She heard the clank of the trailer tail gate being lowered outside.

"Because you have to be cracked to get up at that

167

hour." Stewart Ames grinned, a bright twinkle in his eyes. "Or else in love."

A beaming smile spread immediately across her face. "Is that right!" Brandy laughed. Blowing him a quick kiss, she darted out of the door.

The liver-colored sorrel was tied to the outside of the trailer, saddled and bridled, his four white feet clearly visible in the dim early morning light. With ears pricked, the horse turned to watch Brandy's approach.

Jim threw the last bolt to refasten the tail gate in place. "Good morning."

"Good morning," Brandy returned the greeting.

"Are you ready?"

"My horse is saddled and waiting at the stable around the back," she answered. Her heart quickened at the warm way his gaze ran over her. The reins were pulled free of the slip-knot that tied them to the trailer and Jim fell into step beside Brandy, leading his horse around to the rear of the house.

Dawn was streaking the eastern horizon when they mounted and rode off toward the empty desert. The comfortable creak of saddle leather filled the sage-scented air. The gray Arabian Brandy rode pranced a little, tossing his dish-shaped head, showing off in front of his quieter equine partner.

"It's peaceful, isn't it?" she said as the pale golden sunrise reached out to embrace more of the sky.

"Very," Jim agreed.

They rode on in silence, enjoying the quiet birthing

of a new day. It came softly, the golden light building to orange, the purpling sky lightening to blue, then the golden sun rising slowly above the horizon. There was nothing about it to resemble the blaze of glory that was sundown.

At the knoll of a hill, Jim reined in his horse. As Brandy glimpsed the panorama of desert spread before her, she did the same.

"I never tire of this," she said, knowing he felt the same affinity for the desert.

Hooking a faded denimed leg around the saddle horn, Jim leaned forward in his saddle, his expression relaxed and at ease. His dark gaze didn't pause in its slow surveillance of the land.

"This land helps keep the right perspective on life. In the desert, man is just a humble creature. Material possessions become immaterial. All the money in the world couldn't duplicate this scene," he stated, then glanced at Brandy, a wry smile tugging the corners of his hard mouth. "In my work, that's a valuable thing to remember."

"Then it's more than just a desire for privacy that brings you out here in the desert," she observed.

Jim shrugged lazily. "I suppose there are a lot of reasons if I ever took the time to think of them all." He unhooked his leg. "Shall we ride on?"

At Brandy's nod, they set off at a trot. "How long will you be filming here in Tucson?" She swerved her horse around a growth of prickly pear cactus, then back alongside the sorrel.

169

"A month at the most."

"And then?"

"Back to Los Angeles to wrap it up." His dark eyes squinted towards the sun, as if measuring the hour by its height.

The thought that in less than a month he might be gone didn't sit well. It was inevitable that he had to leave some time, but she didn't really want to think about what it would mean to her.

"When the movie's finished, what are you going to do?" she asked instead.

"I've signed to do another movie. Filming will start as soon as this one is completed. It will be the end of the year before I have any free time, and not then if Don has his way." He was silent, the gap filled by the muffled thud of the horses' hooves on the gravelly sand and the creaky moans of the saddles. With a flash of perception, Jim voiced the answer to the question Brandy was just thinking. "None of the movies calls for any location shots in Arizona."

"Oh." It was a very tired sound. Determinedly she raised her chin. "You travel a lot, don't you? It must be fun to see so many different parts of the world."

"I've always enjoyed traveling before." His qualifying reply made her glance curiously at him. Jim held her gaze for a searching second, then looked ahead. "I've never had any reason except the ranch to hurry back."

What did that mean? He had accused her of talking in riddles, yet he was doing it.

"And now?" she queried.

"And now I think it's time we were heading back to your house." The grooves around his mouth deepened.

He knew he had deliberately misunderstood her question. Brandy guessed it was Jim's way of saying he wasn't prepared to answer it now. Was it because of her or LaRaine? Confused, and angered by the confusion, she compressed her lips together in a straight line. Without argument, she followed alongside as he made a half-circle to return.

On impulse, Brandy dug her heels in the gray's flanks. "I'll race you back!" she hurled the challenge over the shoulder as the Arabian bounded forward.

She was three lengths ahead, the Arabian at a gallop, before his sorrel broke out of a trot, stretching his white legs to catch them. The desert was flat and unbroken before them. The two horses and riders raced unchecked through the sage, agilely jumping or dodging the clumps of cactus.

Brandy's horse held the lead, the air rushing past her face and ears. No matter how eagerly she urged Rashad onward, the sorrel kept gaining ground until they were running neck and neck.

Then the sorrel's nose was in front, then his head and neck. In the next stride, Jim reached out and grabbed Brandy's reins beneath the gray's mouth. With uncanny balance and timing, he slowed both horses to a plunging walk before he released the reins.

"We had you for a while!" Brandy declared,

171

breathless from the exhilarating run that had momentarily banished her anger.

"You would have had us again," Jim replied with a laugh. "Pecos can catch almost anything at a quarter of a mile. After that your Arabian would have left him behind."

"That's not fair!" Both horses were blowing and tossing their heads. "You stopped the race when you were ahead," Brandy accused.

"So I did." He edged his horse closer to hers. "That qualifies me as the winner, doesn't it?"

There was a wicked glint in his sliding look. Brandy shook her head in mock exasperation and smiled. "Only because you didn't play fair."

"Everything's fair."

His hand curved around her neck, applying pressure to draw her sideways toward him as he leaned out of his saddle. "It's time for the loser to pay the forfeit," he said. Then his mouth closed warm and firm over hers.

The spark he ignited was just flaming to full life when he moved away. For a breathless instant, Brandy gazed at him, her face glowing, her turquoise eyes sparkling. She laughed, a gay, happy sound. "If I'd known that was the forfeit, I would have lost the race sooner!"

"That's a tempting remark," Jim chuckled.

Although he nudged his mount into a trot, he didn't suggest a second race. Brandy let Rashad join the pace, a prancing lift to his gait compared to the sedate, reaching stride of the quarter horse.

"Unless something unforeseen happens, I'll have a full schedule this week," Jim said after a time. "I'll be working late every night, so I won't be able to see you until probably the weekend. I'll try to call, though."

"That's all right, I understand." But Brandy wished he had said something definite about the weekend instead of leaving her with the feeling that he would fit her in if he could.

Wistfully she remembered that LaRaine would see him every day. Jealously stabbed at her heart, flashing its green shade in her eyes.

CHAPTER NINE

"BRANDY, THE TELEPHONE CALL is for you." Karen walked to the counter, smiling politely to the customer Brandy was helping. "I'll take over here for you." In a secretive gesture, she whispered behind her hand, "It's *him*!"

It took all of Brandy's willpower to walk sedately to the phone, and not race as her heart was doing. After two days, she had almost given up hope that Jim would call.

Taking a quick, calming breath, she picked up the receiver. "Hello."

"Brandy? Jim." He needlessly identified himself. She would have recognized the husky timbre of his voice anywhere. "I hope you don't have any rule against receiving private calls at work."

The warm smile in his voice sent pleasant chills down her spine. "None at all," Brandy assured him.

"Are you free this evening?"

"Yes." There was a skip of her heart.

"I know this is a short notice, but Tom McWade, one of the stuntmen, and Ginny Baker, a director's assistant, drove down to Mexico last night and got married," he explained. "The cast and crew are giving them a party tonight after the day's shooting is over. Will you come?"

Her first reaction was a definite yes, followed immediately by why hadn't he asked LaRaine, or was she to be used in another attempt to make LaRaine jealous?

"Brandy?" His tone questioned her silence.

"Yes, I'm here." Nervously she twined the coiled telephone cord around her finger. "Perhaps you should ask LaRaine instead. She knows everyone and would fit in better than I do."

It was Jim's turn to pause. "If I'd wanted to take LaRaine to the party, I wouldn't have asked you," he said firmly and with a trace of grimness. "Would you like to come or not?"

"Yes—"

"Good. I'll leave word at the gate to expect you between six and seven," he interrupted tersely. "I'm due on the set, so I'll let you get back to work. I'll see you tonight."

Jim didn't wait for her response as he hung up the telephone. Brandy stared at the receiver in her hand, wishing she had refused no matter how much she wanted to see him again.

A FEW MINUTES past six o'clock, she was parked in the lot at Old Tucson. She sat there with the motor off, wishing she had the strength to leave. But it was no use. She had to take the chance that Jim really meant what he said and he did want to take her to the party.

Still apprehensive that she might be being used, she

175

walked into the entrance building. The same balding man was on duty as on her previous visit. His eyes twinkled brightly when he saw her.

"Hello, Miss Ames," he greeted her by name, "I've been expecting you."

She smiled faintly. "Mr. Corbett said he would let you know I was coming."

"He did that." The man held up his hand, signaling for Brandy to wait. He stepped part way out of the door at the rear of the ticket booth and motioned to someone on the other side. Immediately a security guard appeared in cowboy regalia on the other side of the turnstile. "Troy will take you through to the shindig."

Her escort was an older man than Dick Murphy, who had taken her and Karen through before, but he was just as friendly without being inquisitive. He veered away from the center of the western town, leading her toward an area best described as a back lot. From there, Brandy could hear the sound of voices and laughter.

"The party has started already, I take it," she observed with a smile.

"About two hours ago," he agreed, "at least, for those who were finished for the day."

"Are some still working?" By that Brandy meant Jim, but she didn't have to translate.

"Mr. Corbett was wrapping up a scene. It should be finished by now," was the reply.

As they neared the small gathering of celebrators, a

familiar figure separated itself from the group to walk jauntily toward them. Pale blue eyes gleamed mockingly at Brandy.

"Well, well, well. Who have we here?" Bryce Conover demanded in an amused yet jeering tone. "If it isn't the fair-haired little ingénue come to try her luck again!"

"Hello, Mr. Conover." Brandy kept her greeting calm, refusing to react to his baiting words.

"Call me Bryce," he insisted. He flicked an arrogant glance at the guard. "That will be all, Smith. I'll look after Miss Ames."

The man nodded curtly, plainly not liking the autocratic tone. At Brandy's quickly offered thanks, he touched his hat and walked away.

"You didn't have to dismiss him so abruptly," Brandy accused in a low voice. "You could have been more polite."

A sandy brow arched at her censorious tone. "What purpose would it have served?"

"No purpose." Brandy stared at him with frowning astonishment. "It simply would have been polite. Does everything have to have a purpose?"

"Of course." Bryce took her hand and tucked it under his arm, a faint smugness in his smile.

"What purpose is there for you to be nice to me?" Her query was chilled by his insensitivity.

"Ah, it serves a very useful purpose," he assured her.

"Which is?" Brandy prompted.

"LaRaine wants me to keep you entertained."

"Why would you want to do that for her? Are you in love with her or something?" Her hand was clasped too tightly for her to pull it free.

He laughed loudly at the question. "I'm doing it because that raven-haired witch is on her way to the top. Personally I don't think she has the talent to stay there, but she'll make it one way or another. It pays to have friends at the top who owe you. She'll return the favor with interest by suggesting my name for some of the more demanding roles in her future movies."

"That's mercenary," she breathed.

"That's ambition and determination." Bryce smiled down. "Let's walk over to the refreshment bar and get you something to drink."

"I would prefer to find it myself." Brandy tried to prize his fingers from her hand, without success.

"Tonight I'm your shadow. You can't get rid of me, so why not make the best of it?" he cajoled mockingly.

She stopped struggling and glared at him angrily. "No thank you!"

"Are you hoping the rugged James Corbett will come to your rescue?" The sarcasm for such foolish hope was evident in his whispering question.

"He did invite me," she reminded him haughtily.

"Have you asked yourself for what purpose?" jeered Bryce.

At Brandy's hesitation, he laughed and led her toward the small crowd. It had grown steadily since her arrival and they were forced to queue up at the bar. She refused the champagne Bryce tried to persuade her to take, requesting the iced fruit drink instead.

The drink did enable her to free her hand from his grasp, although he didn't budge from her side. Sipping indifferently at the cold drink, she searched the crowd for Jim. As yet there was no sign of him.

"Forget him and enjoy the party," Bryce murmured.

"Why don't you leave me alone?" she muttered beneath her breath, and smiled politely as she and Bryce were jointly greeted by another couple.

"I couldn't leave you alone and neglected," he chided softly, adding in a louder voice for the other couple's benefit, "Have you met Tom and Marie, Brandy?"

With alacrity he steered her toward the couple, making the introductions when Brandy was forced to plead her ignorance. Bryce made no mention that she was attending the party as Jim's date, and she found it difficult to assert her true role.

There was consolation that the other couple's presence eliminated Bryce's sarcastically mocking comments, but that relief was nearly negated by his arm that had leisurely drifted around her waist. No matter how discreetly she tried to shift away from his hold, Bryce succeeded in keeping her in reach.

Pressure was applied to her waist to bring her closer to his side. Brandy had been smiling agreement with a comment from Marie, and she kept the expression on her face as she glanced at Bryce, the anger flashing in her eyes expressing her displeasure and distaste for his action.

Before she could subtly twist some space between them, Jim spoke behind her. "I'm glad to see you've been enjoying yourself until I arrived."

Whirling about, she saw the cynical hardness in his dark eyes and guessed at the construction he had made of the preceding minutes. LaRaine was with him, her diamond-black eyes sparking in malicious satisfaction. A combination of anger and embarrassment flamed Brandy's cheeks.

"Really, darling," Bryce chided mockingly, "you shouldn't look so guilty. Jim will think there's something going on."

Brandy longed to slap the arrogant look off his face, but enough interested looks had already been aroused for her to want to draw more attention. She decided the best thing to do was ignore everything.

"Are you all finished for the day, Jim?" she asked as pleasantly and evenly as she could.

"Yes, I am."

"You mean it's finally a print on that love scene between you and LaRaine?" Bryce arched a sandy brow in disbelief.

"Yes," LaRaine flashed an intimate smile at Jim, who was still aloofly inspecting Brandy's tautly controlled expression. "After nearly all day, we finally got it right."

The thought of Jim being in LaRaine's arms all day

180

made Brandy's stomach churn. It was too easy to visualize those two equally dark heads locked in a passionate kiss.

"Excuse us, LaRaine," Jim stated briskly, "it's time Brandy and I found the bride and groom and offered them our best wishes."

His announcement was unexpected. Brandy had not thought he would want to deprive himself of LaRaine's company, or at least not so soon. LaRaine appeared just as surprised and not at all pleased.

Instead of protesting, LaRaine smiled. "Tell Ginny I'll see her later, will you?"

"Of course," Jim nodded.

Brandy started to step forward, but at the same moment Bryce took hold of her wrist and partially extended her hand toward Jim.

"I give her back to your care, Jim," Bryce drawled.

As he released her wrist, he exerted just enough pressure to tip the glass in her hand. Brandy gasped at the sudden shock of ice-cold liquid spilling down her front. Blinking in surprise, she stared at the purpling wetness staining the front of her lime-green dress.

"Bryce, you fool!" LaRaine cried angrily, taking a handkerchief Jim had removed from his pocket. "How could you be so clumsy!"

Marie took the nearly empty glass from Brandy's hand while LaRaine dabbed uselessly at the spreading stain on her front. Brandy found the actress's concern for her appearance hard to believe, yet LaRaine was actually trying to help.

"I certaily didn't do it on purpose!" Bryce protested vigorously.

"Why don't you think once before pulling some childish stunt like that?" LaRaine snapped, grimacing as she looked at the futility of her efforts. "It's going to leave a horrid spot when it dries. Maybe we could rinse it out with some cold water." She turned to Jim. "Your trailer is the closest. Is it all right with you if we use it?"

"Here's the key." He took it from his pocket and handed it to LaRaine.

"Can I help?" Marie offered as LaRaine started to lead a bewildered Brandy away.

"No, Brandy and I can manage," the actress refused with a dismissing smile.

A travel trailer parked along the side of the backlot was their destination. LaRaine inserted the key in the lock and opened the door, holding it for Brandy to precede her inside.

"There's a bedroom in the rear," the brunette instructed. "You can slip your dress off there while I run some cold water in the sink."

Brandy started down the narrow hallway, suddenly wondering if she had misjudged LaRaine all this time. She had been so blinded by jealously that she hadn't wanted to see that the stunningly beautiful woman could be kind and thoughtful.

"LaRaine, I don't know how to ... to thank you," Brandy faltered in her confusion. "I mean, your helping me and all."

182

"It's nothing." The water tap was turned on in the sink.

Unzipping her dress, Brandy pulled it over her head. There was fortunately only a small stain on her undergarments. LaRaine stepped into the narrow hall.

"Hand me your dress." She held out her hand, taking the dress when Brandy gave it. "By the way," LaRaine added over her shoulder, "in the closet on your right, one of my robes is hanging on the hook."

Opening the door, Brandy saw the scarlet satin robe and the few clean shirts and slacks belonging to Jim. A bitter taste coated her tongue. The veil of pretense fell away, and Brandy knew exactly why LaRaine had been so kind. Now she even had doubts if the accident had been genuine or planned.

The whole object had been for Brandy to discover LaRaine's robe in Jim's trailer. It wasn't hidden away, but relatively out in the open. With that scarlet red color, Jim must have seen it was there; he must have accepted it as natural. Which meant that he and La-Raine were lovers. LaRaine wanted Brandy convinced of that beyond any lingering doubt.

Something died inside her. Mechanically Brandy slipped on the scarlet robe, and the coolly silky material slid over her bare skin. As she tied the sash, Brandy saw LaRaine framed in the hallway, arms crossed in front of her, a feline look on her face.

"Aren't you going to ask about the robe?" La-Raine purred.

Brandy jerked the knot of the sash tight, tossing her

head back proudly. "Is that what you want?"

"I though you might wonder about finding it here," the brunnette shrugged.

"Why should I?" Brandy returned, walking determinedly past the woman to the sinkful of water and her stained dress lying beside it. "I've always guessed you wanted Jim."

"I mean to have him," LaRaine declared.

"I think you phrased that wrong." Brandy picked up her dress, trembling hands squeezing the excess water out of the sponge before she tried to rinse away the stain. "Shouldn't you have said I love him?"

"Naturally I do. We make a perfect couple, in many ways."

Bryce's comment earlier that evening gave Brandy a fresh insight into that remark. "What you mean is that Jim's talent and reputation would carry you a long way up the ladder, isn't it?" she accused coldly. Maybe Jim never had been and never would be hers, but she didn't intend to let the calculating actress walk all over her without scoring a few blows. "I happen to love Jim Corbett the man. Who do you love—the celebrity James Corbett?"

"What a quaint turn of phrase!" LaRaine laughed, a harsh, unfriendly sound. "Fortunately the two are intertwined. When you get one, you automatically have the other. And he's mine."

"If that's the case, then why are you so worried about me?" Brandy challenged.

"You remind me of my cousin." Venom dripped

184

from LaRaine's voice. "She pretended to be all sweetness and innocence, too, but the first chance she had, she proved how devious she could be. I'm not going to give you the chance to spoil things."

"It's a pity he doesn't see you for what you are," Brandy declared with open disgust. "Maybe he had. Maybe that's why he's been taking me out."

"We quarreled. He only asked you out to make me jealous," LaRaine jeered. "Only a few minutes ago he was telling me that he was sorry he had asked you to come here tonight. He decided he would plead tiredness and take you home early. If you want to save yourself some embarrassment, you'll take my advice and leave now. You can use the accident to your dress as an excuse."

Stubbornly Brandy kept dabbing away at the stain with the sponge. "You'd like me to do that, wouldn't you?"

"You stupid little chit!"

"That's enough, LaRaine." The door had opened silently and Jim stepped inside, his broad-shouldered frame filling the small trailer.

LaRaine recovered from her astonishment more swiftly than Brandy, laughing brightly and walking toward him. She didn't appear unnerved by the harshness of his expression as Brandy was.

"Jim," she spoke his name in a delighted voice, "Brandy and I were just—"

"I know what you were just doing," he interrupted coldly. "I was listening outside."

That statement caused the stunning brunette to falter. She glanced angrily at Brandy as if she blamed her. "I suppose you're going to take that conniving little witch's side against me," she cried, with venom and bitterness in her voice.

"You've made a grave mistake, LaRaine," was his even reply, "you've begun to believe what you read in the gossip columns."

"But you and I—" she protested.

"There never has been a "you and I" except in your publicity agent's imagination. You came to me saying that you needed some newspaper exposure to help your career, and I agreed to take part in the publicity. That's all there ever was between us," Jim stated, and Brandy wanted to cry with relief. "Now, I suggest that you get out of my trailer before I throw you out."

Her ego wounded, LaRaine seethed in silent outrage an instant longer, then with a contemptuous toss of her raven hair, she stalked past him to the door, slamming it as she walked out.

For the first time, Jim turned to Brandy. The hard mouth crooked at the corners as he ran a quick eye over the scarlet robe she was wearing.

"That isn't your color," he observed dryly.

Unconsciously, one hand moved to the satiny front. "It was hanging in the closet," Brandy swallowed, her heart hammering in her ears with joy.

"LaRaine wore it to protect one of her costumes today. I remembered she'd left it here when she

186

stopped at lunch to give me the new script rewrites. If I remembered it, I knew she had," Jim explained, 'and I guessed what she would let you think."

"I'm afraid I believed it." There wasn't that much distance between them in the small trailer, but he closed it with unbearable slowness.

He took the sponge from her hand and tossed it in the sink. "Would you care to repeat the statement you made earlier?"

"Which one?" Her breath was stolen by the smoldering light in his dark eyes.

His gaze burned over her face in possession. "The one about loving someone."

Brandy swayed closer, her hands warmly clasped between his. "I—I'm in love with you, Jim." The catch in her funny little voice said she couldn't help herself.

"In that case, you won't object if I tell you we're getting married in August." A slow, lazy smile softened his hard features.

Brandy caught back the little sob of supreme happiness. "That's so long to wait."

"I want to be very sure, darling." His fingers reached out to gently caress the outline of her cheek. "I want you to be as certain of your love for me as I am of mine for you."

Tears shimmered turquoise bright. "I am."

The dark head bent toward hers, the masculine mouth murmuring against the softness of her lips. "I love you."

Surrendering to the possession of his kiss, Brandy wound her arms around his neck, returning his love with unrestrained joy. The Sonora sundown blazed through the trailer windows, flaming over their embrace.

Poignant tales of love, conflict, romance and adventure

Harlequin Presents...

Elegant and sophisticated novels of
great romantic fiction . . .
12 All time best sellers.

Join the millions of avid Harlequin readers all over the world who delight in the magic of a really exciting novel.

From the library of Harlequin Presents all time best sellers — we are proud and pleased to make available the 12 selections listed here.

Combining all the essential elements you expect of great story telling, and bringing together your very favourite authors — you'll thrill to these exciting tales of love, conflict, romance, sophistication and adventure. You become involved with characters who are interesting, vibrant, and alive. Their individual conflicts, struggles, needs, and desires, grip you, the reader, until the final page.

Have you missed any of these *Harlequin Presents...*

Offered to you in the sequence in which they were originally printed — this is an opportunity for you to add to your Harlequin Presents . . . library.

This elegant and sophisticated series was first introduced in 1973, and has been a huge success ever since. The world's top romantic fiction authors combine glamour, exotic locales dramatic and poignant love themes woven into gripping and absorbing plots to create an unique reading experience in each novel.

You'd expect to pay $1.75 or more for this calibre of best selling novel, — at only **$1.25 each**, Harlequin Presents are truly top value, top quality entertainment.

Don't delay — order yours today

Complete and mail this coupon today!

ORDER FORM

Harlequin Reader Service

In U.S.A.:
MPO Box 707,
Niagara Falls, N.Y. 14302

In Canada:
649 Ontario St., Stratford,
Ontario N5A 6W2

Please send me the following Harlequin Presents . . . I am
enclosing my check or money order for $1.25 for each
novel ordered, plus 25¢ to cover postage and handling.

Number of novels checked _____ @ $1.25 each = $ _____

N.Y. and N.J. residents add appropriate sales tax $ _____

Postage and handling $ _.25_

TOTAL $ _____

NAME _____
(Please Print)

ADDRESS _____

CITY _____

STATE / PROV. _____ ZIP / POSTAL CODE

PRS 239

Offer expires December 31, 1978